NATHANIEL HAWTHORNE (July 4, 1804 – May 19, 1864) was an American novelist and short story writer. His works often focus on history, morality, and religion.

Nathaniel Hawthorne

AN OLD WOMAN'S TALE

AND OTHER WRITINGS

DELHI OPEN BOOKS

**AN OLD WOMAN'S TALE
AND OTHER WRITINGS
by NATHANIEL HAWTHORNE**

Edition copyright © Delhi Open Books, 2023

Published by

Delhi Open Books

G/F, 4771/23, Bharat Ram Road, Daryaganj, New Delhi-110002
Ph.: 91-11-42408081
E-mail: **delhiopenbooks2016@gmail.com**

ISBN: 978-81-961623-9-9

Cover, Typesetting, and Book Design by **ROHIT**

Contents

An Old Woman's Tale

In the house where I was born, there used to be an old woman crouching all day long over the kitchen fire, with her elbows on her knees and her feet in the ashes. Once in a while she took a turn at the spit, and she never lacked a coarse gray stocking in her lap, the foot about half finished; it tapered away with her own waning life, and she knit the toe-stitch on the day of her death. She made it her serious business and sole amusement to tell me stories at any time from morning till night, in a mumbling, toothless voice, as I sat on a log of wood, grasping her check-apron in both my hands. Her personal memory included the better part of a hundred years, and she had strangely jumbled her own experience and observation with those of many old people who died in her young days; so that she might have been taken for a contemporary of Queen Elizabeth, or of John Rogers in the Primer. There are a thousand of her traditions lurking in the corners and by-places of my mind, some more marvellous than what is to follow, some less so, and a few not marvellous in the least, all of which I should like to repeat, if I were as happy as she in having a listener. But I am humble enough to own, that I do not deserve a listener half so well as that old toothless woman, whose narratives possessed an excellence attributable neither to herself, nor to any single individual. Her ground-plots, seldom within the widest scope of probability, were filled up with homely and natural incidents, the gradual accretions of a long course of years, and fiction hid its grotesque extravagance in this garb of truth, like the Devil (an appropriate simile, for the old woman supplies it) disguising himself, cloven-foot and all, in mortal attire. These tales generally referred to her birthplace, a village in the valley of the Connecticut, the aspect of which she impressed with great vividness on my fancy. The houses in that tract of country, long a wild and dangerous frontier, were rendered defensible by a strength of architecture that has preserved many of them till our own times, and I cannot describe the sort of pleasure with which, two summers since, I rode through the little town in question, while one object after another rose familiarly to my eye, like successive portions of a dream becoming realized. Among other things equally probable, she was wont to assert that all the inhabitants of this village (at certain intervals, but whether of twenty-five or fifty years, or a whole century, remained a disputable point) were subject to a simultaneous slumber, continuing one hour's space. When that mysterious time arrived, the parson snored over his half-written sermon, though it were Saturday night and no provision made for the morrow,—the mother's eyelids closed as she bent over her infant, and no childish cry awakened,— the watcher at the bed of mortal sickness slumbered upon the death-pillow, and the dying man anticipated his sleep of ages by one as deep and dreamless. To speak emphatically, there was a soporific influence throughout the village, stronger than if every mother's son and daughter were reading a dull story; notwithstanding which the old woman professed to hold the substance of the ensuing account from one of those principally concerned in it.

One moonlight summer evening, a young man and a girl sat down together in the open air. They were distant relatives, sprung from a stock once wealthy, but of late years so poverty-stricken, that David had not a penny to pay the marriage fee, if Esther should consent to wed. The seat they had chosen was in an open grove of elm and walnut trees, at a right angle of the road; a spring of diamond water just bubbled into the moonlight beside them, and then whimpered away through the bushes and long grass, in search of a neighboring millstream. The nearest house (situate within twenty yards of them, and the residence of their great-grandfather in his lifetime) was a venerable old edifice, crowned with many high and narrow peaks, all overrun by innumerable creeping plants, which hung curling about the roof like a nice young wig on an elderly gentleman's head. Opposite to this establishment was a tavern, with a well and horse-trough before it, and a low green bank running along the left side of the door. Thence, the road went onward, curving scarce perceptibly, through the village, divided in the midst by a narrow lane of verdure, and bounded on each side by a grassy strip of twice its own breadth. The houses had generally an odd look. Here, the moonlight tried to get a glimpse of one, a rough old heap of ponderous timber, which, ashamed of its dilapidated aspect, was hiding behind a great thick tree; the lower story of the next had sunk almost under ground, as if the poor little house were a-weary of the world, and retiring into the seclusion of its own cellar; farther on stood one of the few recent structures, thrusting its painted face conspicuously into the street, with an evident idea that it was the fairest thing there. About midway in the village was a grist-mill, partly concealed by the descent of the ground towards the stream which turned its wheel. At the southern extremity, just so far distant that the window-paces dazzled into each other, rose the meeting-house, a dingy old barn-like building, with an enormously disproportioned steeple sticking up straight into heaven, as high as the Tower of Babel, and the cause of nearly as much confusion in its day. This steeple, it must be understood, was an afterthought, and its addition to the main edifice, when the latter had already begun to decay, had excited a vehement quarrel, and almost a schism in the church, some fifty years before. Here the road wound down a hill and was seen no more, the remotest object in view being the graveyard gate, beyond the meetinghouse. The youthful pair sat hand in hand beneath the trees, and for several moments they had not spoken, because the breeze was hushed, the brook scarce tinkled, the leaves had ceased their rustling, and everything lay motionless and silent as if Nature were composing herself to slumber.

"What a beautiful night it is, Esther!" remarked David, somewhat drowsily.

"Very beautiful," answered the girl, in the same tone.

"But how still!" continued David.

"Ah, too still!" said Esther, with a faint shudder, like a modest leaf when the wind kisses it.

Perhaps they fell asleep together, and, united as their spirits were by close and tender sympathies, the same strange dream might have wrapped them in its shadowy arms. But they conceived, at the time, that they still remained wakeful by the spring of bubbling water, looking down through the village, and all along the moonlighted road, and at the queer old houses, and at the trees which thrust their great twisted branches almost into the windows. There was only a sort of mistiness over their minds like the smoky air of an early autumn night. At length, without any vivid astonishment, they became conscious that a great many people were either entering the village or already in the street, but whether they came from the meeting-house, or from a little beyond it, or where the devil they came from, was more than could be determined. Certainly, a crowd of people seemed to be there, men, women, and children, all of whom were yawning and rubbing their eyes, stretching their limbs, and staggering from side to side of the road, as if but partially awakened from a sound slumber. Sometimes they stood stock-still, with their hands over their brows to shade their sight from the moonbeams. As they drew near, most of their countenances appeared familiar to Esther and David, possessing the peculiar features of families in the village, and that general air and aspect by which a person would recognize his own townsmen in the remotest ends of the earth. But though the whole multitude might have been taken, in the mass, for neighbors and acquaintances, there was not a single individual whose exact likeness they had ever before seen. It was a noticeable circumstance, also, that the newest fashioned garment on the backs of these people might have been worn by the great-grandparents of the existing generation. There was one figure behind all the rest, and not yet near enough to be perfectly distinguished.

"Where on earth, David, do all these odd people come from?" said Esther, with a lazy inclination to laugh.

"Nowhere on earth, Esther," replied David, unknowing why he said so.

As they spoke, the strangers showed some symptoms of disquietude, and looked towards the fountain for an instant, but immediately appeared to assume their own trains of thought and previous purposes. They now separated to different parts of the village, with a readiness that implied intimate local knowledge, and it may be worthy of remark, that, though they were evidently loquacious among themselves, neither their footsteps nor their voices reached the ears of the beholders. Wherever there was a venerable old house, of fifty years' standing and upwards, surrounded by its elm or walnut trees, with its dark and weather-beaten barn, its well, its orchard and stone-walls, all ancient and all in good repair around it, there a little group of these people assembled. Such parties were mostly composed of an aged man and woman, with the younger members of a family; their faces were full of joy, so deep that it assumed the shade of melancholy; they pointed to each other the minutest objects about the homesteads, things in their hearts, and were now comparing them with the originals. But where hollow places by the wayside, grass-grown and uneven, with unsightly chimneys rising ruinous in the midst, gave indications of a fallen dwelling and of hearths long cold, there did a few of the strangers sit them down on the mouldering beams, and on the yellow moss that had overspread the door-stone. The men folded their arms, sad and speechless; the women wrung their hands with a more vivid expression of grief; and the little children tottered to their knees, shrinking away from the open grave of domestic love. And wherever a recent edifice reared its white and flashy front on the foundation of an old one, there a gray-haired man might be seen to shake his staff in anger at it, while his aged dame and their offspring appeared to join in their maledictions, forming a fearful picture in the ghostly moon light. While these scenes were passing, the one figure in the rear of all the rest was descending the hollow towards the mill, and the eyes of David and Esther were drawn thence to a pair with whom they could fully sympathize. It was a youth in a sailor's dress and a pale slender maiden, who met each other with a sweet embrace in the middle of the street.

"How long it must be since they parted," observed David.

"Fifty years at least," said Esther.

They continued to gaze with unwondering calmness and quiet interest, as the dream (if such it were) unrolled its quaint and motley semblance before them, and their notice was now attracted by several little knots of people apparently engaged in conversation. Of these one of the earliest collected and most characteristic was near the tavern, the persons who composed it being seated on the low green bank along the left side of the door. A conspicuous figure here was a fine corpulent old fellow in his shirt-sleeves and flame-colored breeches, and with a stained white apron over his paunch, beneath which he held his hands and wherewith at times be wiped his ruddy face. The stately decrepitude of one of his companions, the scar of an Indian tomahawk on his crown, and especially his worn buff coat, were appropriate marks of a veteran belonging to an old Provincial garrison, now deaf to the roll-call. Another showed his rough face under a tarry hat and wore a pair of wide trousers, like an ancient mariner who bad tossed away his youth upon the sea, and was returned, hoary and weather-beaten, to his inland home. There was also a thin young man, carelessly dressed, who ever and anon cast a sad look towards the pale maiden above mentioned. With these there sat a hunter, and one or two others, and they were soon joined by a miller, who came upward from the dusty mill, his coat as white as if besprinkled with powdered starlight. All these (by the aid of jests, which might indeed be old, but had not been recently repeated) waxed very merry, and it was rather strange, that just as their sides shook with the heartiest laughter, they appeared greatly like a group of shadows flickering in the moonshine. Four personages, very different from these, stood in front of the large house with its periwig of creeping plants. One was a little elderly figure, distinguished by the gold on his three-cornered bat and sky-blue coat, and by the seal of arms annexed to his great gold watch-chain; his air and aspect befitted a Justice of Peace and County Major, and all earth's pride and pomposity were squeezed into this small gentleman of five feet high. The next in importance was a grave person of sixty or seventy years, whose black suit and hand sufficiently indicated his character, and the polished baldness of whose head was worthy of a famous preacher in the village, half a century before, who had made wigs a subject of pulpit denunciation. The two other figures, both clad in dark gray, showed the sobriety of Deacons; one was ridiculously tall and thin, like a man of ordinary bulk infinitely produced, as the mathematicians say; while the brevity and thickness of his colleague seemed a compression of the same man. These four talked with great earnestness, and their gestures intimated that they had revived the ancient dispute about the meeting-house steeple. The grave person in black spoke with composed solemnity, as if he were addressing a Synod; the short deacon grunted out occasional sentences, as brief as himself; his tall brother drew the long thread of his argument through the whole discussion, and (reasoning from analogy) his voice must indubitably have been small and squeaking. But the little old man in gold-lace was evidently scorched by his own red-hot eloquence; he bounced from one to another, shook his cane at the steeple, at the two deacons, and almost in the parson's face, stamping with his foot fiercely enough to break a hole through the very earth; though, indeed, it could not exactly be said that the green grass bent beneath him. The figure, noticed as coming behind all the rest, had now surmounted the ascent from the mill, and proved to be an elderly lady with something in her hand.

"Why does she walk so slow?" asked David.

"Don't you see she is lame?" said Esther.

This gentlewoman, whose infirmity had kept her so far in the rear of the crowd, now came hobbling on, glided unobserved by the polemic group, and paused on the left brink of the fountain, within a few feet of the two spectators. She was a magnificent old dame, as ever mortal eye beheld. Her spangled shoes and gold-clocked stockings shone gloriously within the spacious circle of a red hoop-petticoat, which swelled to the very point of explosion, and was bedecked all over with embroidery a little tarnished. Above the petticoat, and parting in front so as to display it to the best advantage, was a figured blue damask gown. A wide and stiff ruff encircled her neck, a cap of the finest muslin, though rather dingy, covered her head; and her nose was bestridden by a pair of gold-bowed spectacles with enormous glasses. But the old lady's face was pinched, sharp and sallow, wearing a niggardly and avaricious expression, and forming an odd contrast to the splendor of her attire, as did likewise the implement which she held in her hand. It was a sort of iron shovel (by housewives termed a "slice"), such as is used in clearing the oven, and with this, selecting a spot between a walnut-tree and the fountain, the good dame made an earnest attempt to dig. The tender sods, however, possessed a strange impenetrability. They resisted her efforts like a quarry of living granite, and losing her breath, she cast down the shovel and seemed to bemoan herself most piteously, gnashing her teeth (what few she had) and wringing her thin yellow hands. Then, apparently with new

   An Old Woman's Tale and other writings

hope, she resumed her toil, which still had the same result,—a circumstance the less surprising to David and Esther, because at times they would catch the moonlight shining through the old woman, and dancing in the fountain beyond. The little man in goldlace now happened to see her, and made his approach on tiptoe.

"How hard this elderly lady works!" remarked David.

"Go and help her, David," said Esther, compassionately.

As their drowsy void spoke, both the old woman and the pompous little figure behind her lifted their eyes, and for a moment they regarded the youth and damsel with something like kindness and affection; which, however, were dim and uncertain, and passed away almost immediately. The old woman again betook herself to the shovel, but was startled by a hand suddenly laid upon her shoulder; she turned round in great trepidation, and beheld the dignitary in the blue coat; then followed an embrace of such closeness as would indicate no remoter connection than matrimony between these two decorous persons. The gentleman next pointed to the shovel, appearing to inquire the purpose of his lady's occupation; while she as evidently parried his interrogatories, maintaining a demure and sanctified visage as every good woman ought, in similar cases. Howbeit, she could not forbear looking askew, behind her spectacles, towards the spot of stubborn turf. All the while, their figures had a strangeness in them, and it seemed as if some cunning jeweller had made their golden ornaments of the yellowest of the setting sunbeams, and that the blue of their garments was brought from the dark sky near the moon, and that the gentleman's silk waistcoat was the bright side of a fiery cloud, and the lady's scarlet petticoat a remnant of the blush of morning,—and that they both were two unrealities of colored air. But now there was a sudden movement throughout the multitude. The Squire drew forth a watch as large as the dial on the famous steeple, looked at the warning hands and got him gone, nor could his lady tarry; the party at the tavern door took to their heels, headed by the fat man in the flaming breeches; the tall deacon stalked away immediately, and the short deacon waddled after, making four steps to the yard; the mothers called their children about them and set forth, with a gentle and sad glance behind. Like cloudy fantasies that hurry by a viewless impulse from the sky, they all were fled, and the wind rose up and followed them with a strange moaning down the lonely street. Now whither these people went, is more than may be told; only David and Esther seemed to see the shadowy splendor of the ancient dame, as she lingered in the moonshine at the graveyard gate, gazing backward to the fountain.

"O Esther! I have had such a dream!" cried David, starting up, and rubbing his eyes.

"And I such another!" answered Esther, gaping till her pretty red lips formed a circle.

"About an old woman with gold-bowed spectacles," continued David.

"And a scarlet hoop-petticoat," added Esther. They now stared in each other's eyes, with great astonishment and some little fear. After a thoughtful moment or two, David drew a long breath and stood upright.

"If I live till to-morrow morning," said he, "I'll see what may be buried between that tree and the spring of water."

"And why not to-night, David?" asked Esther; for she was a sensible little girl, and bethought herself that the matter might as well be done in secrecy.

David felt the propriety of the remark and looked round for the means of following her advice. The moon shone brightly on something that rested against the side of the old house, and, on a nearer view, it proved to be an iron shovel, bearing a singular resemblance to that which they had seen in their dreams. He used it with better success than the old woman, the soil giving way so freely to his efforts, that he had soon scooped a hole as large as the basin of the spring. Suddenly, he poked his head down to the very bottom of this cavity. "Oho!—what have we here?" cried David.

A Rill from the Town-Pump

Noon by the north clock! Noon by the east! High noon, too, by these hot sunbeams, which full, scarcely aslope, upon my head and almost make the water bubble and smoke in the trough under my nose. Truly, we public characters have a tough time of it! And among all the town-officers chosen at March meeting, where is he that sustains for a single year the burden of such manifold duties as are imposed in perpetuity upon the town-pump? The title of "town-treasurer" is rightfully mine, as guardian of the best treasure that the town has. The overseers of the poor ought to make me their chairman, since I provide bountifully for the pauper without expense to him that pays taxes. I am at the head of the fire department and one of the physicians to the board of health. As a keeper of the peace all water-drinkers will confess me equal to the constable. I perform some of the duties of the town-clerk by promulgating public notices when they are posted on my front. To speak within bounds, I am the chief person of the municipality, and exhibit, moreover, an admirable pattern to my brother-officers by the cool, steady, upright, downright and impartial discharge of my business and the constancy with which I stand to my post. Summer or winter, nobody seeks me in vain, for all day long I am seen at the busiest corner, just above the market, stretching out my arms to rich and poor alike, and at night I hold a lantern over my head both to show where I am and keep people out of the gutters. At this sultry noontide I am cupbearer to the parched populace, for whose benefit an iron goblet is chained to my waist. Like a dramseller on the mall at muster-day, I cry aloud to all and sundry in my plainest accents and at the very tiptop of my voice.

Here it is, gentlemen! Here is the good liquor! Walk up,

 An Old Woman's Tale and other writings

walk up, gentlemen! Walk up, walk up! Here is the superior stuff! Here is the unadulterated ale of Father Adam—better than Cognac, Hollands, Jamaica, strong beer or wine of any price; here it is by the hogshead or the single glass, and not a cent to pay! Walk up, gentlemen, walk up, and help yourselves!

It were a pity if all this outcry should draw no customers. Here they come.—A hot day, gentlemen! Quaff and away again, so as to keep yourselves in a nice cool sweat.—You, my friend, will need another cupful to wash the dust out of your throat, if it be as thick there as it is on your cowhide shoes. I see that you have trudged half a score of miles to-day, and like a wise man have passed by the taverns and stopped at the running brooks and well-curbs. Otherwise, betwixt heat without and fire within, you would have been burnt to a cinder or melted down to nothing at all, in the fashion of a jelly-fish. Drink and make room for that other fellow, who seeks my aid to quench the fiery fever of last night's potations, which he drained from no cup of mine.—Welcome, most rubicund sir! You and I have been great strangers hitherto; nor, to confess the truth, will my nose be anxious for a closer intimacy till the fumes of your breath be a little less potent. Mercy on you, man! the water absolutely hisses down your red-hot gullet and is converted quite to steam in the miniature Tophet which you mistake for a stomach. Fill again, and tell me, on the word of an honest toper, did you ever, in cellar, tavern, or any kind of a dram-shop, spend the price of your children's food for a swig half so delicious? Now, for the first time these ten years, you know the flavor of cold water. Good-bye; and whenever you are thirsty, remember that I keep a constant supply at the old stand.—Who next?—Oh, my little friend, you are let loose from school and come hither to scrub your blooming face and drown the memory of certain taps of the ferule, and other schoolboy troubles, in a draught from the town-pump? Take it, pure as the current of your young life. Take it, and may your heart and tongue never be scorched with a fiercer thirst than now! There, my dear child! put down the cup and yield your place to this elderly gentleman who treads so tenderly over the paving-stones that I suspect he is afraid of breaking them. What! he limps by without so much as thanking me, as if my hospitable offers were meant only for people who have no wine-cellars.—Well, well, sir, no harm done, I hope? Go draw the cork, tip the decanter; but when your great toe shall set you a-roaring, it will be no affair of mine. If gentlemen love the pleasant titillation of the gout, it is all one to the town-pump. This thirsty dog with his red tongue lolling out does not scorn my hospitality, but stands on his hind legs and laps eagerly out of the trough. See how lightly he capers away again!—Jowler, did your worship ever have the gout?

Are you all satisfied? Then wipe your mouths, my good friends, and while my spout has a moment's leisure I will delight the town with a few historical remniscences. In far antiquity, beneath a darksome shadow of venerable boughs, a spring bubbled out of the leaf-strewn earth in the very spot where you now behold me on the sunny pavement. The water was as bright and clear and deemed as precious as liquid diamonds. The Indian sagamores drank of it from time immemorial till the fatal deluge of the firewater burst upon the red men and swept their whole race away from the cold fountains. Endicott and his followers came next, and often knelt down to drink, dipping their long beards in the spring. The richest goblet then was of birch-bark. Governor Winthrop, after a journey afoot from Boston, drank here out of the hollow of his hand. The elder Higginson here wet his palm and laid it on the brow of the first town-born child. For many years it was the watering-place, and, as it were, the washbowl, of the vicinity, whither all decent folks resorted to purify their visages and gaze at them afterward—at least, the pretty maidens did—in the mirror which it made. On Sabbath-days, whenever a babe was to be baptized, the sexton filled his basin here and placed it on the communion-table of the humble meeting-house, which partly covered the site of yonder stately brick one. Thus one generation after another was consecrated to Heaven by its waters, and cast their waxing and waning shadows into its glassy bosom, and vanished from the earth, as if mortal life were but a flitting image in a fountain. Finally the fountain vanished also. Cellars were dug on all sides and cart-loads of gravel flung upon its source, whence oozed a turbid stream, forming a mud-puddle at the corner of two streets. In the hot months, when its refreshment was most needed, the dust flew in clouds over the forgotten birthplace of the waters, now their grave. But in the course of time a town-pump was sunk into the source of the ancient spring; and when the first decayed, another took its place, and then another, and still another, till here stand I, gentlemen and ladies, to serve you with my iron goblet. Drink and be refreshed. The water is as pure and cold as that which slaked the thirst of the red sagamore beneath the aged boughs, though now the gem of the wilderness is treasured under these hot stones, where no shadow falls but from the brick buildings. And be it the moral of my story that, as this wasted and long-lost fountain is now known and prized again, so shall the virtues of cold water—too little valued since your fathers' days—be recognized by all.

Your pardon, good people! I must interrupt my stream of eloquence and spout forth a stream of water to replenish the trough for this teamster and his two yoke of oxen, who have come from Topsfield, or somewhere along that way. No part of my business is pleasanter than the watering of cattle. Look! how rapidly they lower the water-mark on the sides of the trough, till their capacious stomachs are moistened with a gallon or two apiece and they can afford time to breathe it in with sighs of calm enjoyment. Now they roll their quiet eyes around the brim of their monstrous drinking-vessel. An ox is your true toper.

But I perceive, my dear auditors, that you are impatient for the remainder of my discourse. Impute it, I beseech you, to no defect of modesty if I insist a little longer on so fruitful a topic as my own multifarious merits. It is altogether for your good. The better you think of me, the better men and women you will find yourselves. I shall say nothing of my all-important aid on washing-days, though on that account alone I might call myself the household god of a hundred families. Far be it from me, also, to hint, my respectable friends, at the show of dirty faces which you would present without my pains to keep you clean. Nor will I remind you how often, when the midnight bells make you tremble for your combustible town, you have fled to the town-pump and found me always at my post firm amid the confusion and ready to drain my vital current in your behalf. Neither is it worth while to lay much stress on my claims to a medical diploma as the physician whose simple rule of practice is preferable to all the nauseous lore which has found men sick, or left them so, since the days of Hippocrates. Let us take a broader view of my beneficial influence on mankind.

No; these are trifles, compared with the merits which wise men concede to me—if not in my single self, yet as the representative of a class—of being the grand reformer of the age. From my spout, and such spouts as mine, must flow the stream that shall cleanse our earth of the vast portion of its crime and anguish which has gushed from the fiery fountains of the still. In this mighty enterprise the cow shall be my great confederate. Milk and water—the TOWN-PUMP and the Cow! Such is the glorious copartnership that shall tear down the distilleries and brewhouses, uproot the vineyards, shatter the cider-presses, ruin the tea and coffee trade, and finally monopolize the whole business of quenching thirst. Blessed consummation! Then Poverty shall pass away from the land, finding no hovel so wretched where her squalid form may shelter herself. Then Disease, for lack of other victims, shall gnaw its own heart and die. Then Sin, if she do not die, shall lose half her strength. Until now the frenzy of hereditary fever has raged in the human blood, transmitted from sire to son

   An Old Woman's Tale and other writings

and rekindled in every generation by fresh draughts of liquid flame. When that inward fire shall be extinguished, the heat of passion cannot but grow cool, and war—the drunkenness of nations—perhaps will cease. At least, there will be no war of households. The husband and wife, drinking deep of peaceful joy—a calm bliss of temperate affections—shall pass hand in hand through life and lie down not reluctantly at its protracted close. To them the past will be no turmoil of mad dreams, nor the future an eternity of such moments as follow the delirium of the drunkard. Their dead faces shall express what their spirits were and are to be by a lingering smile of memory and hope.

Ahem! Dry work, this speechifying, especially to an unpractised orator. I never conceived till now what toil the temperance lecturers undergo for my sake; hereafter they shall have the business to themselves.—Do, some kind Christian, pump a stroke or two, just to wet my whistle.—Thank you, sir!—My dear hearers, when the world shall have been regenerated by my instrumentality, you will collect your useless vats and liquor-casks into one great pile and make a bonfire in honor of the town-pump. And when I shall have decayed like my predecessors, then, if you revere my memory, let a marble fountain richly sculptured take my place upon this spot. Such monuments should be erected everywhere and inscribed with the names of the distinguished champions of my cause. Now, listen, for something very important is to come next.

There are two or three honest friends of mine—and true friends I know they are—who nevertheless by their fiery pugnacity in my behalf do put me in fearful hazard of a broken nose, or even a total overthrow upon the pavement and the loss of the treasure which I guard.—I pray you, gentlemen, let this fault be amended. Is it decent, think you, to get tipsy with zeal for temperance and take up the honorable cause of the town-pump in the style of a toper fighting for his brandy-bottle?

Or can the excellent qualities of cold water be no otherwise exemplified than by plunging slapdash into hot water and woefully scalding yourselves and other people? Trust me, they may. In the moral warfare which you are to wage—and, indeed, in the whole conduct of your lives—you cannot choose a better example than myself, who have never permitted the dust and sultry atmosphere, the turbulence and manifold disquietudes, of the world around me to reach that deep, calm well of purity which may be called my soul. And whenever I pour out that soul, it is to cool earth's fever or cleanse its stains.

One o'clock! Nay, then, if the dinner-bell begins to speak, I may as well hold my peace. Here comes a pretty young girl of my acquaintance with a large stone pitcher for me to fill. May she draw a husband while drawing her water, as Rachel did of old!—Hold out your vessel, my dear! There it is, full to the brim; so now run home, peeping at your sweet image in the pitcher as you go, and forget not in a glass of my own liquor to drink "SUCCESS TO THE TOWN-PUMP."

     An Old Woman's Tale and other writings

Benjamin Franklin

Born 1706. Died 1790.

In the year 1716, or about that period, a boy used to be seen in the streets of Boston, who was known among his schoolfellows and playmates by the name of Ben Franklin. Ben was born in 1706; so that he was now about ten years old. His father, who had come over from England, was a soap-boiler and tallow-chandler, and resided in Milk Street, not far from the old South Church.

Ben was a bright boy at his book, and even a brighter one when at play with his comrades. He had some remarkable qualities which always seemed to give him the lead, whether at sport or in more serious matters. I might tell you a number of amusing anecdotes about him. You are acquainted, I suppose, with his famous story of the WHISTLE, and how he bought it with a whole pocketful of coppers, and afterwards repented of his bargain. But Ben had grown a great boy since those days, and had gained wisdom by experience; for it was one of his peculiarities, that no incident ever happened to him without teaching him some valuable lesson. Thus he generally profited more by his misfortunes, than many people do by the most favorable events that could befall them.

Ben's face was already pretty well known to the inhabitants of Boston. The selectmen, and other people of note, often used to visit his father, for the sake of talking about the affairs of the town or province. Mr. Franklin was considered a person of great wisdom and integrity, and was respected by all who knew him, although he supported his family by the humble trade of boiling soap, and making tallow-candles.

While his father and the visitors were holding deep

consultations about public affairs, little Ben would sit on his stool in a corner, listening with the greatest interest, as if he understood every word. Indeed, his features were so full of intelligence, that there could be but little doubt, not only that he understood what was said, but that he could have expressed some very sagacious opinions out of his own mind. But, in those days, boys were expected to be silent in the presence of their elders. However, Ben Franklin was looked upon as a very promising lad, who would talk and act wisely by and by.

"Neighbor Franklin," his father's friends would sometimes say, "you ought to send this boy to college and make a minister of him."

"I have often thought of it," his father would reply; "and my brother Benjamin promises to give him a great many volumes of manuscript sermons in case he should be educated for the church. But I have a large family to support, and cannot afford the expense."

In fact, Mr. Franklin found it so difficult to provide bread for his family, that, when the boy was ten years old, it became necessary to take him from school. Ben was then employed in cutting candlewicks into equal lengths, and filling the moulds with tallow; and many families in Boston spent their evenings by the light of the candles which he had helped to make. Thus, you see, in his early days, as well as in his manhood his labors contributed to throw light upon dark matters.

Busy as his life now was, Ben still found time to keep company with his former schoolfellows. He and the other boys were very fond of fishing, and spent any of their leisure hours on the margin of the mill-pond, catching flounders, perch, eels, and tom-cod, which came up thither with the tide. The place where they fished is now, probably, covered with stone-pavements and brick buildings, and thronged with people, and with vehicles of all kinds. But, at that period, it was a marshy spot on the outskirts of the town, where gulls flitted and screamed overhead, and salt meadow-grass grew under foot. On the edge of the water there was a deep bed of clay, in which the boys were forced to stand, while they caught their fish. Here they dabbled in mud and mire like a flock of ducks.

"This is very uncomfortable," said Ben Franklin one day to his comrades, while they were standing mid-leg deep in the quagmire.

"So it is," said the other boys. "What a pity we have no better place to stand!"

If it had not been for Ben, nothing more would have been done or said about the matter. But it was not in his nature to be sensible of an inconvenience, without using his best efforts to find a remedy. So, as he and his comrades were returning from the water-side, Ben suddenly threw down his string of fish with a very determined air:

"Boys," cried he, "I have thought of a scheme, which will be greatly for our benefit, and for the public benefit!"

It was queer enough, to be sure, to hear this little chap— this rosy-cheeked, ten-year-old boy—talking about schemes for the public benefit! Nevertheless, his companions were ready to listen, being assured that Ben's scheme, whatever it was, would be well worth their attention. They remembered how sagaciously he had conducted all their enterprises, ever since he had been old enough to wear small-clothes.

They remembered, too, his wonderful contrivance of sailing across the mill-pond by lying flat on his back, in the water, and allowing himself to be drawn along by a paper-kite. If Ben could do that, he might certainly do any thing.

"What is your scheme, Ben?—what is it?" cried they all.

It so happened that they had now come to a spot of ground where a new house was to be built. Scattered round about lay a great many large stones, which were to be used for the cellar and foundation. Ben mounted upon the highest of these stones, so that he might speak with the more authority.

"You know, lads," said he, "what a plague it is, to be forced to stand in the quagmire yonder—over shoes and stockings (if we wear any) in mud and water. See! I am bedaubed to the knees of my small-clothes, and you are all in the same pickle. Unless we can find some remedy for this evil, our fishing-business must be entirely given up. And, surely, this would be a terrible misfortune!"

"That it would!—that it would!" said his comrades, sorrowfully.

"Now I propose," continued Master Benjamin, "that we build a wharf, for the purpose of carrying on our fisheries. You see these stones. The workmen mean to use them for the underpinning of a house; but that would be for only one man's advantage. My plan is to take these same stones, and carry them to the edge of the water and build a wharf with them. This will not only enable us to carry on the fishing business with comfort, and to better advantage, but it will likewise be a great convenience to boats passing up and down the stream. Thus, instead of one man, fifty, or a hundred, or a thousand, besides ourselves, may be benefited by these stones. What say you, lads?—shall we build the wharf?"

Ben's proposal was received with one of those uproarious shouts, wherewith boys usually express their delight at whatever completely suits their views. Nobody thought of questioning the right and justice of building a wharf, with stones that belonged to another person.

"Hurrah, hurrah!" shouted they. "Let's set about it!"

It was agreed that they should all be on the spot, that evening, and commence their grand public enterprise by moonlight. Accordingly, at the appointed time, the whole gang of youthful laborers assembled, and eagerly began to remove

   An Old Woman's Tale and other writings

the stones. They had not calculated how much toil would be requisite, in this important part of their undertaking. The very first stone which they laid hold of, proved so heavy, that it almost seemed to be fastened to the ground. Nothing but Ben Franklin's cheerful and resolute spirit could have induced them to persevere.

Ben, as might be expected, was the soul of the enterprise. By his mechanical genius, he contrived methods to lighten the labor of transporting the stones; so that one boy, under his directions, would perform as much as half a dozen, if left to themselves. Whenever their spirits flagged, he had some joke ready, which seemed to renew their strength by setting them all into a roar of laughter. And when, after an hour or two of hard work, the stones were transported to the water-side, Ben Franklin was the engineer, to superintend the construction of the wharf.

The boys, like a colony of ants, performed a great deal of labor by their multitude, though the individual strength of each could have accomplished but little. Finally, just as the moon sank below the horizon, the great work was finished.

"Now, boys," cried Ben, "let's give three cheers, and go home to bed. To-morrow, we may catch fish at our ease!" "Hurrah! hurrah! hurrah!" shouted his comrades.

Then they all went home, in such an ecstasy of delight that they could hardly get a wink of sleep.

The story was not yet finished; but George's impatience caused him to interrupt it.

"How I wish that I could have helped to build that wharf!" exclaimed he. "It must have been glorious fun. Ben Franklin for ever, say I!"

"It was a very pretty piece of work," said Mr. Temple. "But wait till you hear the end of the story."

"Father," inquired Edward, "whereabouts in Boston was the mill-pond, on which Ben built his wharf?"

"I do not exactly know," answered Mr. Temple; "but I suppose it to have been on the northern verge of the town, in the vicinity of what are now called Merrimack and Charlestown streets. That thronged portion of the city was once a marsh. Some of it, in fact, was covered with water."

[As the children had no more questions to ask, Mr. Temple proceeded to relate what consequences ensued from the building of Ben Franklin's wharf.]

In the morning, when the early sunbeams were gleaming on the steeples and roofs of the town, and gilding the water that surrounded it, the masons came, rubbing their eyes, to begin their work at the foundation of the new house. But, on reaching the spot, they rubbed their eyes so much the harder. What had become of their heap of stones!

"Why, Sam," said one to another, in great perplexity, "here's been some witchcraft at work, while we were asleep. The stones must have flown away through the air!"

"More likely they have been stolen!" answered Sam.

"But who on earth would think of stealing a heap of stones?" cried a third. "Could a man carry them away in his pocket?"

The master-mason, who was a gruff kind of man, stood scratching his head, and said nothing, at first. But, looking carefully on the ground, he discerned innumerable tracks of little feet, some with shoes, and some barefoot. Following these tracks with his eye, he saw that they formed a beaten path towards the water-side.

"Ah, I see what the mischief is," said he, nodding his head. "Those little rascals, the boys! they have stolen our stones to build a wharf with!"

The masons immediately went to examine the new structure. And to say the truth, it was well worth looking at, so neatly, and with such admirable skill, had it been planned and finished. The stones were put together so securely, that there was no danger of their being loosened by the tide, however swiftly it might sweep along. There was a broad and safe platform to stand upon, whence the little fishermen might cast their lines into deep water, and draw up fish in abundance. Indeed, it almost seemed as if Ben and his comrades might be forgiven for taking the stones, because they had done their job in such a workmanlike manner.

"The chaps, that built this wharf, understood their business pretty well," said one of the masons. "I should not be ashamed of such a piece of work myself."

But the master-mason did not seem to enjoy the joke. He was one of those unreasonable people, who care a great deal more for their own rights and privileges, than for the convenience of all the rest of the world.

"Sam," said he, more gruffly than usual, "go call a constable."

So Sam called a constable, and inquiries were set on foot to discover the perpetrators of the theft. In the course of the day, warrants were issued, with the signature of a Justice of the Peace, to take the bodies of Benjamin Franklin and other evil-disposed persons, who had stolen a heap of stones. If the owner of the stolen property had not been more merciful than the master-mason, it might have gone hard with our friend Benjamin and his fellow-laborers. But, luckily for them, the gentleman had a respect for Ben's father, and moreover, was amused with the spirit of the whole affair. He therefore let the culprits off pretty easily.

But, when the constables were dismissed, the poor boys had to go through another trial, and receive sentence, and suffer execution too, from their own fathers. Many a rod I grieve to say, was worn to the stump, on that unlucky night.

As for Ben, he was less afraid of a whipping than of his father's disapprobation. Mr. Franklin, as I have mentioned before, was a sagacious man, and also an inflexibly upright one. He had read much, for a person in his rank of life, and had pondered upon the ways of the world, until he had gained more wisdom than a whole library of books could have taught him. Ben had a greater reverence for his father, than for any other person in the world, as well on account of his spotless integrity, as of his practical sense and deep views of things.

Consequently, after being released from the clutches of the law, Ben came into his father's presence, with no small perturbation of mind.

"Benjamin, come hither," began Mr. Franklin, in his customary solemn and weighty tone.

The boy approached, and stood before his father's chair, waiting reverently to hear what judgment this good man would pass upon his late offence. He felt that now the right and wrong of the whole matter would be made to appear.

"Benjamin," said his father, "what could induce you to take property which did not belong to you?"

"Why, father," replied Ben, hanging his head, at first, but then lifting his eyes to Mr. Franklin's face, "if it had been merely for my own benefit, I never should have dreamed of it. But I knew that the wharf would be a public convenience. If the owner of the stones should build a house with them, nobody will enjoy any advantage except himself. Now, I made use of them in a way that was for the advantage of many persons. I thought it right to aim at doing good to the greatest number."

"My son," said Mr. Franklin, solemnly, "so far as it was in your power, you have done a greater harm to the public, than

                    An Old Woman's Tale and other writings

to the owner of the stones."

"How can that be, father?" asked Ben.

"Because," answered his father, "in building your wharf with stolen materials, you have committed a moral wrong. There is no more terrible mistake, than to violate what is eternally right, for the sake of a seeming expediency. Those who act upon such a principle, do the utmost in their power to destroy all that is good in the world."

"Heaven forbid!" said Benjamin.

"No act," continued Mr. Franklin, "can possibly be for the benefit of the public generally, which involves injustice to any individual. It would be easy to prove this by examples. But, indeed, can we suppose that our all-wise and just Creator would have so ordered the affairs of the world, that a wrong act should be the true method of attaining a right end? It is impious to think so! And I do verily believe, Benjamin, that almost all the public and private misery of mankind arises from a neglect of this great truth—that evil can produce only evil—that good ends must be wrought out by good means."

"I will never forget it again," said Benjamin, bowing his head.

"Remember," concluded his father, "that, whenever we vary from the highest rule of right, just so far we do an injury to the world. It may seem otherwise for the moment; but, both in Time and in Eternity, it will be found so."

To the close of his life, Ben Franklin never forgot this conversation with his father; and we have reason to suppose, that in most of his public and private career, he endeavored to act upon the principles which that good and wise man had then taught him.

After the great event of building the wharf, Ben continued to cut wick-yarn and fill candle-moulds for about two years.

But, as he had no love for that occupation, his father often took him to see various artisans at their work, in order to discover what trade he would prefer. Thus Ben learned the use of a great many tools, the knowledge of which afterwards proved very useful to him. But he seemed much inclined to go to sea. In order to keep him at home, and likewise to gratify his taste for letters, the lad was bound apprentice to his elder brother, who had lately set up a printing-office in Boston.

Here he had many opportunities of reading new books, and of hearing instructive conversation. He exercised himself so successfully in writing composition, that, when no more than thirteen or fourteen years old, he became a contributor to his brother's newspaper. Ben was also a versifier, if not a poet. He made two doleful ballads; one about the shipwreck of Captain Worthilake, and the other about the pirate Black Beard, who not long before, infested the American seas.

When Ben's verses were printed, his brother sent him to sell them to the town's-people, wet from the press. "Buy my ballads!" shouted Benjamin, as he trudged through the streets, with a basketful on his arm. "Who'll buy a ballad about Black Beard? A penny a piece! a penny a piece! who'll buy my ballads?"

If one of those roughly composed and rudely printed ballads could be discovered now, it would be worth more than its weight in gold.

In this way our friend Benjamin spent his boyhood and youth, until, on account of some disagreement with his brother, he left his native town and went to Philadelphia. He landed in the latter city, a homeless and hungry young man, and bought three-pence worth of bread to satisfy his appetite. Not knowing where else to go, he entered a Quaker meeting-house, sat down, and fell fast asleep. He has not told us whether his slumbers were visited by any dreams. But it would have been a strange dream, indeed, and an incredible one, that should have

     An Old Woman's Tale and other writings

foretold how great a man he was destined to become, and how much he would be honored in that very city, where he was now friendless, and unknown.

So here we finish our story of the childhood of Benjamin Franklin. One of these days, if you would know what he was in his manhood, you must read his own works, and the history of American Independence.

"Do let us hear a little more of him!" said Edward; "not that I admire him so much as many other characters; but he interests me, because he was a Yankee boy."

"My dear son," replied Mr. Temple, "it would require a whole volume of talk, to tell you all that is worth knowing about Benjamin Franklin. There is a very pretty anecdote of his flying a kite in the midst of a thunder-storm, and thus drawing down the lightning from the clouds, and proving that it was the same thing as electricity. His whole life would be an interesting story, if we had time to tell it."

"But, pray, dear father, tell us what made him so famous," said George. "I have seen his portrait a great many times. There is a wooden bust of him in one of our streets, and marble ones, I suppose, in some other places. And towns, and ships of war, and steamboats, and banks, and academies, and children, are often named after Franklin. Why should he have grown so very famous?"

"Your question is a reasonable one, George," answered his father. "I doubt whether Franklin's philosophical discoveries, important as they were, or even his vast political services, would have given him all the fame which he acquired. It appears to me that Poor Richard's Almanac did more than any thing else towards making him familiarly known to the public. As the writer of those proverbs, which Poor Richard was supposed to utter, Franklin became the counsellor and household friend of almost every family in America. Thus, it was the humblest of all his labors that has done the most for his fame."

"I have read some of those proverbs," remarked Edward; "but I do not like them. They are all about getting money, or saving it."

"Well," said his father, "they were suited to the condition of the country; and their effect, upon the whole, has doubtless been good,—although they teach men but a very small portion of their duties."

Chippings with a Chisel

Passing a summer several years since at Edgartown, on the island of Martha's Vineyard, I became acquainted with a certain carver of tombstones who had travelled and voyaged thither from the interior of Massachusetts in search of professional employment. The speculation had turned out so successful that my friend expected to transmute slate and marble into silver and gold to the amount of at least a thousand dollars during the few months of his sojourn at Nantucket and the Vineyard. The secluded life and the simple and primitive spirit which still characterizes the inhabitants of those islands, especially of Martha's Vineyard, insure their dead friends a longer and dearer remembrance than the daily novelty and revolving bustle of the world can elsewhere afford to beings of the past. Yet, while every family is anxious to erect a memorial to its departed members, the untainted breath of Ocean bestows such health and length of days upon the people of the isles as would cause a melancholy dearth of business to a resident artist in that line. His own monument, recording his decease by starvation, would probably be an early specimen of his skill. Gravestones, therefore, have generally been an article of imported merchandise.

In my walks through the burial-ground of Edgartown—where the dead have lain so long that the soil, once enriched by their decay, has returned to its original barrenness—in that ancient burial-ground I noticed much variety of monumental sculpture. The elder stones, dated a century back or more, have borders elaborately carved with flowers and are adorned with a multiplicity of death's-heads, crossbones, scythes, hour-glasses, and other lugubrious emblems of mortality, with here and there a winged cherub to direct the mourner's spirit upward. These productions of Gothic taste must have been quite beyond the colonial skill of the day, and were probably carved in London and brought across the ocean to commemorate the defunct worthies of this lonely isle. The more recent monuments are mere slabs of slate in the ordinary style, without any superfluous flourishes to set off the bald inscriptions. But others—and those far the most impressive both to my taste and feelings—were roughly hewn from the gray rocks of the island, evidently by the unskilled hands of surviving friends and relatives. On some there were merely the initials of a name; some were inscribed with misspelt prose or rhyme, in deep letters which the moss and wintry rain of many years had not been able to obliterate. These, these were graves where loved ones slept. It is an old theme of satire, the falsehood and vanity of monumental eulogies; but when affection and sorrow grave the letters with their own painful labor, then we may be sure that they copy from the record on their hearts.

My acquaintance the sculptor—he may share that title with Greenough, since the dauber of signs is a painter as well as Raphael—had found a ready market for all his blank slabs of marble and full occupation in lettering and ornamenting them. He was an elderly man, a descendant of the old Puritan family of Wigglesworth, with a certain simplicity and singleness both of heart and mind which, methinks, is more rarely found among us Yankees than in any other community of people. In spite of his gray head and wrinkled brow, he was quite like a child in all matters save what had some reference to his own business; he seemed, unless my fancy misled me, to view mankind in no other relation than as people in want of tombstones, and his literary attainments evidently comprehended very little either of prose of poetry which had not at one time or other been inscribed on slate or marble. His sole task and office among the immortal pilgrims of the tomb—the duty for which Providence had sent the old man into the world, as it were with a chisel in his hand—was to label the dead bodies, lest

     An Old Woman's Tale and other writings

their names should be forgotten at the resurrection. Yet he had not failed, within a narrow scope, to gather a few sprigs of earthly, and more than earthly, wisdom—the harvest of many a grave. And, lugubrious as his calling might appear, he was as cheerful an old soul as health and integrity and lack of care could make him, and used to set to work upon one sorrowful inscription or another with that sort of spirit which impels a man to sing at his labor. On the whole, I found Mr. Wigglesworth an entertaining, and often instructive, if not an interesting, character; and, partly for the charm of his society, and still more because his work has an invariable attraction for "man that is born of woman," I was accustomed to spend some hours a day at his workshop. The quaintness of his remarks and their not infrequent truth—a truth condensed and pointed by the limited sphere of his view—gave a raciness to his talk which mere worldliness and general cultivation would at once have destroyed.

Sometimes we would discuss the respective merits of the various qualities of marble, numerous slabs of which were resting against the walls of the shop, or sometimes an hour or two would pass quietly without a word on either side while I watched how neatly his chisel struck out letter after letter of the names of the Nortons, the Mayhews, the Luces, the Daggets, and other immemorial families of the Vineyard. Often with an artist's pride the good old sculptor would speak of favorite productions of his skill which were scattered throughout the village graveyards of New England. But my chief and most instructive amusement was to witness his interviews with his customers, who held interminable consultations about the form and fashion of the desired monuments, the buried excellence to be commemorated, the anguish to be expressed, and finally the lowest price in dollars and cents for which a marble transcript of their feelings might be obtained. Really, my mind received many fresh ideas which perhaps may remain in it even longer than Mr. Wigglesworth's hardest marble will retain the deepest strokes of his chisel.

An elderly lady came to bespeak a monument for her first love, who had been killed by a whale in the Pacific Ocean no less than forty years before. It was singular that so strong an impression of early feeling should have survived through the changes of her subsequent life, in the course of which she had been a wife and a mother, and, so far as I could judge, a comfortable and happy woman. Reflecting within myself, it appeared to me that this lifelong sorrow—as, in all good faith, she deemed it—was one of the most fortunate circumstances of her history. It had given an ideality to her mind; it had kept her purer and less earthy than she would otherwise have been by drawing a portion of her sympathies apart from earth. Amid the throng of enjoyments and the pressure of worldly care and all the warm materialism of this life she had communed with a vision, and had been the better for such intercourse. Faithful to the husband of her maturity, and loving him with a far more real affection than she ever could have felt for this dream of her girlhood, there had still been an imaginative faith to the ocean-buried; so that an ordinary character had thus been elevated and refined. Her sighs had been the breath of Heaven to her soul. The good lady earnestly desired that the proposed monument should be ornamented with a carved border of marine plants interwined with twisted sea-shells, such as were probably waving over her lover's skeleton or strewn around it in the far depths of the Pacific. But, Mr. Wigglesworth's chisel being inadequate to the task, she was forced to content herself with a rose hanging its head from a broken stem.

After her departure I remarked that the symbol was none of the most apt.

"And yet," said my friend the sculptor, embodying in this image the thoughts that had been passing through my own mind, "that broken rose has shed its sweet smell through forty years of the good woman's life."

It was seldom that I could find such pleasant food for contemplation as in the above instance. None of the applicants, I think, affected me more disagreeably than an old man who came, with his fourth wife hanging on his arm, to bespeak gravestones for the three former occupants of his marriage-bed. I watched with some anxiety to see whether his remembrance of either were more affectionate than of the other two, but could discover no symptom of the kind. The three monuments were all to be of the same material and form, and each decorated in bas-relief with two weeping willows, one of these sympathetic trees bending over its fellow, which was to be broken in the midst and rest upon a sepulchral urn. This, indeed, was Mr. Wigglesworth's standing emblem of conjugal bereavement. I shuddered at the gray polygamist who had so utterly lost the holy sense of individuality in wedlock that methought he was fain to reckon upon his fingers how many women who had once slept by his side were now sleeping in their graves. There was even—if I wrong him, it is no great matter—a glance sidelong at his living spouse, as if he were inclined to drive a thriftier bargain by bespeaking four gravestones in a lot.

I was better pleased with a rough old whaling-captain who gave directions for a broad marble slab divided into two compartments, one of which was to contain an epitaph on his deceased wife and the other to be left vacant till death should engrave his own name there. As is frequently the case among the whalers of Martha's Vineyard, so much of this storm-beaten widower's life had been tossed away on distant seas that out of twenty years of matrimony he had spent scarce three, and those at scattered intervals, beneath his own roof. Thus the wife of his youth, though she died in his and her declining age, retained the bridal dewdrops fresh around her memory.

My observations gave me the idea, and Mr. Wigglesworth confirmed it, that husbands were more faithful in setting up memorials to their dead wives than widows to their dead husbands. I was not ill-natured enough to fancy that women less than men feel so sure of their own constancy as to be willing to give a pledge of it in marble. It is more probably the fact that, while men are able to reflect upon their lost companions as remembrances apart from themselves, women, on the other hand, are conscious that a portion of their being has gone with the departed whithersoever he has gone. Soul clings to soul, the living dust has a sympathy with the dust of the grave; and by the very strength of that sympathy the wife of the dead shrinks the more sensitively from reminding the world of its existence. The link is already strong enough; it needs no visible symbol. And, though a shadow walks ever by her side and the touch of a chill hand is on her bosom, yet life, and perchance its natural yearnings, may still be warm within her and inspire her with new hopes of happiness. Then would she mark out the grave the scent of which would be perceptible on the pillow of the second bridal? No, but rather level its green mound with the surrounding earth, as if, when she dug up again her buried heart, the spot had ceased to be a grave.

Yet, in spite of these sentimentalities, I was prodigiously amused by an incident of which I had not the good-fortune to be a witness, but which Mr. Wigglesworth related with considerable humor. A gentlewoman of the town, receiving news of her husband's loss at sea, had bespoken a handsome slab of marble, and came daily to watch the progress of my friend's chisel. One afternoon, when the good lady and the sculptor were in the very midst of the epitaph—which the departed spirit might have been greatly comforted to read— who should walk into the workshop but the deceased himself, in substance as well as spirit! He had been picked up at sea, and stood in no present need of tombstone or epitaph.

"And how," inquired I, "did his wife bear the shock of joyful surprise?"

"Why," said the old man, deepening the grin of a death's-head on which his chisel was just then employed, "I really felt for the poor woman; it was one of my best pieces of marble— and to be thrown away on a living man!"

A comely woman with a pretty rosebud of a daughter came to select a gravestone for a twin-daughter, who had died a month before. I was impressed with the different nature of their feelings for the dead. The mother was calm and woefully resigned, fully conscious of her loss, as of a treasure which she had not always possessed, and therefore had been aware that it might be taken from her; but the daughter evidently had no real knowledge of what Death's doings were. Her thoughts knew, but not her heart. It seemed to me that by the print and pressure which the dead sister had left upon the survivor's spirit her feelings were almost the same as if she still stood side by side and arm in arm with the departed, looking at the slabs of marble, and once or twice she glanced around with a sunny smile, which, as its sister-smile had faded for ever, soon grew confusedly overshadowed. Perchance her consciousness was truer than her reflection; perchance her dead sister was a closer companion than in life.

The mother and daughter talked a long while with Mr. Wigglesworth about a suitable epitaph, and finally chose an ordinary verse of ill-matched rhymes which had already been inscribed upon innumerable tombstones. But when we ridicule the triteness of monumental verses, we forget that Sorrow reads far deeper in them than we can, and finds a profound and individual purport in what seems so vague and inexpressive unless interpreted by her. She makes the epitaph anew, though the selfsame words may have served for a thousand graves.

"And yet," said I afterward to Mr. Wigglesworth, "they might have made a better choice than this. While you were discussing the subject I was struck by at least a dozen simple and natural expressions from the lips of both mother and daughter. One of these would have formed an inscription equally original and appropriate."

"No, no!" replied the sculptor, shaking his head; "there is a good deal of comfort to be gathered from these little old scraps of poetry, and so I always recommend them in preference to any new-fangled ones. And somehow they seem to stretch to suit a great grief and shrink to fit a small one."

It was not seldom that ludicrous images were excited by what took place between Mr. Wigglesworth and his customers. A shrewd gentlewoman who kept a tavern in the town was anxious to obtain two or three gravestones for the deceased members of her family, and to pay for these solemn commodities by taking the sculptor to board. Hereupon a fantasy arose in my mind of good Mr. Wigglesworth sitting down to dinner at a broad, flat tombstone carving one of his own plump little marble cherubs, gnawing a pair of crossbones and drinking out of a hollow death's-head or perhaps a lachrymatory vase or sepulchral urn, while his hostess's dead children waited on him at the ghastly banquet. On communicating this nonsensical picture to the old man he laughed heartily and pronounced my humor to be of the right sort.

"I have lived at such a table all my days," said he, "and eaten no small quantity of slate and marble."

"Hard fare," rejoined I, smiling, "but you seemed to have found it excellent of digestion, too."

A man of fifty or thereabouts with a harsh, unpleasant countenance ordered a stone for the grave of his bitter enemy, with whom he had waged warfare half a lifetime, to their mutual misery and ruin. The secret of this phenomenon was that hatred had become the sustenance and enjoyment of the poor wretch's soul; it had supplied the place of all kindly affections; it had been really a bond of sympathy between himself and the man who shared the passion; and when its object died, the unappeasable foe was the only mourner for the dead. He expressed a purpose of being buried side by side with his enemy.

"I doubt whether their dust will mingle," remarked the old sculptor to me; for often there was an earthliness in his conceptions.

"Oh yes," replied I, who had mused long upon the incident; "and when they rise again, these bitter foes may find themselves dear friends. Methinks what they mistook for hatred was but love under a mask."

A gentleman of antiquarian propensities provided a memorial for an Indian of Chabbiquidick—one of the few of untainted blood remaining in that region, and said to be a hereditary chieftain descended from the sachem who welcomed Governor Mayhew to the Vineyard. Mr. Wigglesworth exerted his best skill to carve a broken bow and scattered sheaf of arrows in memory of the hunters and warriors whose race was ended here, but he likewise sculptured a cherub, to denote that the poor Indian had shared the Christian's hope of immortality.

"Why," observed I, taking a perverse view of the winged boy and the bow and arrows, "it looks more like Cupid's tomb than an Indian chief's."

"You talk nonsense," said the sculptor, with the offended pride of art. He then added with his usual good-nature, "How can Cupid die when there are such pretty maidens in the Vineyard?"

"Very true," answered I; and for the rest of the day I thought of other matters than tombstones.

At our next meeting I found him chiselling an open book upon a marble headstone, and concluded that it was meant to express the erudition of some black-letter clergyman of the Cotton Mather school. It turned out, however, to be emblematical of the scriptural knowledge of an old woman who had never read anything but her Bible, and the monument was a tribute to her piety and good works from the orthodox church of which she had been a member. In strange contrast with this Christian woman's memorial was that of an infidel whose gravestone, by his own direction, bore an avowal of his belief that the spirit within him would be extinguished like a flame, and that the nothingness whence he sprang would receive him again.

Mr. Wigglesworth consulted me as to the propriety of enabling a dead man's dust to utter this dreadful creed.

"If I thought," said he, "that a single mortal would read the inscription without a shudder, my chisel should never cut a letter of it. But when the grave speaks such falsehoods, the soul of man will know the truth by its own horror."

"So it will," said I, struck by the idea. "The poor infidel may strive to preach blasphemies from his grave, but it will be only another method of impressing the soul with a consciousness of immortality."

There was an old man by the name of Norton, noted throughout the island for his great wealth, which he had accumulated by the exercise of strong and shrewd faculties combined with a most penurious disposition. This wretched miser, conscious that he had not a friend to be mindful of him in his grave, had himself taken the needful precautions for posthumous remembrance by bespeaking an immense slab of white marble with a long epitaph in raised letters, the whole to be as magnificent as Mr. Wigglesworth's skill could make it. There was something very characteristic in this contrivance to have his money's worth even from his own tombstone, which, indeed, afforded him more enjoyment in the few months that he lived thereafter than it probably will in a whole century, now that it is laid over his bones.

This incident reminds me of a young girl—a pale, slender,

feeble creature most unlike the other rosy and healthful damsels of the Vineyard, amid whose brightness she was fading away. Day after day did the poor maiden come to the sculptor's shop and pass from one piece of marble to another, till at last she pencilled her name upon a slender slab which, I think, was of a more spotless white than all the rest. I saw her no more, but soon afterward found Mr. Wigglesworth cutting her virgin-name into the stone which she had chosen.

"She is dead, poor girl!" said he, interrupting the tune which he was whistling, "and she chose a good piece of stuff for her headstone. Now, which of these slabs would you like best to see your own name upon?"

"Why, to tell you the truth, my good Mr. Wigglesworth," replied I, after a moment's pause, for the abruptness of the question had somewhat startled me—"to be quite sincere with you, I care little or nothing about a stone for my own grave, and am somewhat inclined to scepticism as to the propriety of erecting monuments at all over the dust that once was human. The weight of these heavy marbles, though unfelt by the dead corpse or the enfranchised soul, presses drearily upon the spirit of the survivor and causes him to connect the idea of death with the dungeon-like imprisonment of the tomb, instead of with the freedom of the skies. Every gravestone that you ever made is the visible symbol of a mistaken system. Our thoughts should soar upward with the butterfly, not linger with the exuviæ that confined him. In truth and reason, neither those whom we call the living, and still less the departed, have anything to do with the grave."

"I never heard anything so heathenish," said Mr. Wigglesworth, perplexed and displeased at sentiments which controverted all his notions and feelings and implied the utter waste, and worse, of his whole life's labor. "Would you forget your dead friends the moment they are under the sod?"

"They are not under the sod," I rejoined; "then why should

I mark the spot where there is no treasure hidden? Forget them? No; but, to remember them aright, I would forget what they have cast off. And to gain the truer conception of death I would forget the grave."

But still the good old sculptor murmured, and stumbled, as it were, over the gravestones amid which he had walked through life. Whether he were right or wrong, I had grown the wiser from our companionship and from my observations of nature and character as displayed by those who came, with their old griefs or their new ones, to get them recorded upon his slabs of marble. And yet with my gain of wisdom I had likewise gained perplexity; for there was a strange doubt in my mind whether the dark shadowing of this life, the sorrows and regrets, have not as much real comfort in them—leaving religious influences out of the question—as what we term life's joys.

Circe's Palace

Some of you have heard, no doubt, of the wise King Ulysses, and how he went to the siege of Troy, and how, after that famous city was taken and burned, he spent ten long years in trying to get back again to his own little kingdom of Ithaca. At one time in the course of this weary voyage, he arrived at an island that looked very green and pleasant, but the name of which was unknown to him. For, only a little while before he came thither, he had met with a terrible hurricane, or rather a great many hurricanes at once, which drove his fleet of vessels into a strange part of the sea, where neither himself nor any of his mariners had ever sailed. This misfortune was entirely owing to the foolish curiosity of his shipmates, who, while Ulysses lay asleep, had untied some very bulky leathern bags, in which they supposed a valuable treasure to be concealed. But in each of these stout bags, King Aeolus, the ruler of the winds, had tied up a tempest, and had given it to Ulysses to keep in order that he might be sure of a favorable passage homeward to Ithaca; and when the strings were loosened, forth rushed the whistling blasts, like air out of a blown bladder, whitening the sea with foam, and scattering the vessels nobody could tell whither.

Immediately after escaping from this peril, a still greater one had befallen him. Scudding before the hurricane, he reached a place, which, as he afterwards found, was called Laestrygonia, where some monstrous giants had eaten up many of his companions, and had sunk every one of his vessels, except that in which he himself sailed, by flinging great masses of rock at them, from the cliffs along the shore. After going through such troubles as these, you cannot wonder that King Ulysses was glad to moor his tempest-beaten bark in a quiet cove of the green island, which I began with telling you about. But he had encountered so many dangers from giants, and one-eyed Cyclops, and monsters of the sea and land, that he could not help dreading some mischief, even in this pleasant and seemingly solitary spot. For two days, therefore, the poor weather-worn voyagers kept quiet, and either staid on board of their vessel, or merely crept along under the cliffs that bordered the shore; and to keep themselves alive, they dug shellfish out of the sand, and sought for any little rill of fresh water that might be running towards the sea.

Before the two days were spent, they grew very weary of this kind of life; for the followers of King Ulysses, as you will find it important to remember, were terrible gormandizers, and pretty sure to grumble if they missed their regulars meals, and their irregular ones besides. Their stock of provisions was quite exhausted, and even the shellfish began to get scarce, so that they had now to choose between starving to death or venturing into the interior of the island, where perhaps some huge three-headed dragon, or other horrible monster, had his den. Such misshapen creatures were very numerous in those days; and nobody ever expected to make a voyage, or take a journey, without running more or less risk of being devoured by them.

But King Ulysses was a bold man as well as a prudent one; and on the third morning he determined to discover what sort of a place the island was, and whether it were possible to obtain a supply of food for the hungry mouths of his companions. So, taking a spear in his hand, he clambered to the summit of a cliff, and gazed round about him. At a distance, towards the center of the island, he beheld the stately towers of what seemed to be a palace, built of snow-white marble, and rising in the midst of a grove of lofty trees. The thick branches of these trees stretched across the front of the edifice, and more than half concealed it, although, from the portion which he saw, Ulysses judged it to be spacious and exceedingly beautiful, and probably the residence of some great nobleman or prince. A blue smoke went curling up from the chimney, and was almost the pleasantest part of the spectacle to Ulysses. For, from the abundance of this smoke, it was reasonable to conclude that there was a good fire in the kitchen, and that, at dinner-time, a plentiful banquet would be served up to the inhabitants of the palace, and to whatever guests might happen to drop in.

With so agreeable a prospect before him, Ulysses fancied that he could not do better than go straight to the palace gate, and tell the master of it that there was a crew of poor shipwrecked mariners, not far off, who had eaten nothing for a day or two, save a few clams and oysters, and would therefore be thankful for a little food. And the prince or nobleman must be a very stingy curmudgeon, to be sure, if, at least, when his own dinner was over, he would not bid them welcome to the broken victuals from the table.

Pleasing himself with this idea, King Ulysses had made a few steps in the direction of the palace, when there was a great twittering and chirping from the branch of a neighboring tree. A moment afterwards, a bird came flying towards him, and hovered in the air, so as almost to brush his face with its wings. It was a very pretty little bird, with purple wings and body, and yellow legs, and a circle of golden feathers round its neck, and on its head a golden tuft, which looked like a king's crown in miniature. Ulysses tried to catch the bird. But it fluttered nimbly out of his reach, still chirping in a piteous tone, as if it could have told a lamentable story, had it only been gifted with human language. And when he attempted to drive it away, the bird flew no farther than the bough of the next tree, and again came fluttering about his head, with its doleful chirp, as soon as he showed a purpose of going forward.

"Have you anything to tell me, little bird?" asked Ulysses.

And he was ready to listen attentively to whatever the bird

might communicate; for, at the siege of Troy, and elsewhere, he had known such odd things to happen, that he would not have considered it much out of the common run had this little feathered creature talked as plainly as himself.

"Peep!" said the bird, "peep, peep, pe--weep!" And nothing else would it say, but only, "Peep, peep, pe--weep!" in a melancholy cadence, and over and over and over again. As often as Ulysses moved forward, however, the bird showed the greatest alarm, and did its best to drive him back, with the anxious flutter of its purple wings. Its unaccountable behavior made him conclude, at last, that the bird knew of some danger that awaited him, and which must needs be very terrible, beyond all question, since it moved even a little fowl to feel compassion for a human being. So he resolved, for the present, to return to the vessel, and tell his companions what he had seen.

This appeared to satisfy the bird. As soon as Ulysses turned back, it ran up the trunk of a tree, and began to pick insects out of the bark with its long, sharp bill; for it was a kind of woodpecker, you must know, and had to get its living in the same manner as other birds of that species. But every little while, as it pecked at the bark of the tree, the purple bird bethought itself of some secret sorrow, and repeated its plaintive note of "Peep, peep, pe--weep!"

On his way to the shore, Ulysses had the good luck to kill a large stag by thrusting his spear into his back. Taking it on his shoulders (for he was a remarkably strong man), he lugged it along with him, and flung it down before his hungry companions. I have already hinted to you what gormandizers some of the comrades of King Ulysses were. From what is related of them, I reckon that their favorite diet was pork, and that they had lived upon it until a good part of their physical substance was swine's flesh, and their tempers and dispositions were very much akin to the hog. A dish of venison, however,

 An Old Woman's Tale and other writings

was no unacceptable meal to them, especially after feeding so long on oysters and clams. So, beholding the dead stag, they felt of its ribs, in a knowing way, and lost no time in kindling a fire of driftwood, to cook it. The rest of the day was spent in feasting; and if these enormous eaters got up from table at sunset, it was only because they could not scrape another morsel off the poor animal's bones.

The next morning, their appetites were as sharp as ever. They looked at Ulysses, as if they expected him to clamber up the cliff again, and come back with another fat deer upon his shoulders. Instead of setting out, however, he summoned the whole crew together, and told them it was in vain to hope that he could kill a stag every day for their dinner, and therefore it was advisable to think of some other mode of satisfying their hunger.

"Now," said he, "when I was on the cliff, yesterday, I discovered that this island is inhabited. At a considerable distance from the shore stood a marble palace, which appeared to be very spacious, and had a great deal of smoke curling out of one of its chimneys."

"Aha!" muttered some of his companions, smacking their lips. "That smoke must have come from the kitchen fire. There was a good dinner on the spit; and no doubt there will be as good a one to-day."

"But," continued the wise Ulysses, "you must remember, my good friends, our misadventure in the cavern of one-eyed Polyphemus, the Cyclops! Instead of his ordinary milk diet, did he not eat up two of our comrades for his supper, and a couple more for breakfast, and two at his supper again? Methinks I see him yet, the hideous monster, scanning us with that great red eye, in the middle of his forehead, to single out the fattest. And then, again, only a few days ago, did we not fall into the hands of the king of the Laestrygons, and those other horrible giants, his subjects, who devoured a great many more of us than are now left? To tell you the truth, if we go to yonder palace, there can be no question that we shall make our appearance at the dinner table; but whether seated as guests, or served up as food, is a point to be seriously considered."

"Either way," murmured some of the hungriest of the crew; "it will be better than starvation; particularly if one could be sure of being well fattened beforehand, and daintily cooked afterwards."

"That is a matter of taste," said King Ulysses, "and, for my own part, neither the most careful fattening nor the daintiest of cookery would reconcile me to being dished at last. My proposal is, therefore, that we divide ourselves into two equal parties, and ascertain, by drawing lots, which of the two shall go to the palace, and beg for food and assistance. If these can be obtained, all is well. If not, and if the inhabitants prove as inhospitable as Polyphemus, or the Laestrygons, then there will but half of us perish, and the remainder may set sail and escape."

As nobody objected to this scheme, Ulysses proceeded to count the whole band, and found that there were forty-six men, including himself. He then numbered off twenty-two of them, and put Eurylochus (who was one of his chief officers, and second only to himself in sagacity) at their head. Ulysses took command of the remaining twenty-two men, in person. Then, taking off his helmet, he put two shells into it, on one of which was written, "Go," and on the other "Stay." Another person now held the helmet, while Ulysses and Eurylochus drew out each a shell; and the word "Go" was found written on that which Eurylochus had drawn. In this manner, it was decided that Ulysses and his twenty-two men were to remain at the seaside until the other party should have found out what sort of treatment they might expect at the mysterious palace. As there was no help for it, Eurylochus immediately set forth at the head of his twenty-two followers, who went off in a very melancholy state of mind, leaving their friends in hardly better spirits than themselves.

No sooner had they clambered up the cliff, than they discerned the tall marble towers of the palace, ascending, as white as snow, out of the lovely green shadow of the trees which surrounded it. A gush of smoke came from a chimney in the rear of the edifice. This vapor rose high in the air, and, meeting with a breeze, was wafted seaward, and made to pass over the heads of the hungry mariners. When people's appetites are keen, they have a very quick scent for anything savory in the wind.

"That smoke comes from the kitchen!" cried one of them, turning up his nose as high as he could, and snuffing eagerly. "And, as sure as I'm a half-starved vagabond, I smell roast meat in it."

"Pig, roast pig!" said another. "Ah, the dainty little porker. My mouth waters for him."

"Let us make haste," cried the others, "or we shall be too late for the good cheer! "

But scarcely had they made half a dozen steps from the edge of the cliff, when a bird came fluttering to meet them. It was the same pretty little bird, with the purple wings and body, the yellow legs, the golden collar round its neck, and the crown-like tuft upon its head, whose behavior had so much surprised Ulysses. It hovered about Eurylochus, and almost brushed his face with its wings.

"Peep, peep, pe--weep!" chirped the bird.

So plaintively intelligent was the sound, that it seemed as if the little creature were going to break its heart with some mighty secret that it had to tell, and only this one poor note to tell it with.

"My pretty bird," said Eurylochus--for he was a wary

person, and let no token of harm escape his notice--"my pretty bird, who sent you hither? And what is the message which you bring?"

"Peep, peep, pe--weep! " replied the bird, very sorrowfully.

Then it flew towards the edge of the cliff, and looked around at them, as if exceedingly anxious that they should return whence they came. Eurylochus and a few of the others were inclined to turn back. They could not help suspecting that the purple bird must be aware of something mischievous that would befall them at the palace, and the knowledge of which affected its airy spirit with a human sympathy and sorrow. But the rest of the voyagers, snuffing up the smoke from the palace kitchen, ridiculed the idea of returning to the vessel. One of them (more brutal than his fellows, and the most notorious gormandizer in the crew) said such a cruel and wicked thing, that I wonder the mere thought did not turn him into a wild beast, in shape, as he already was in his nature.

"This troublesome and impertinent little fowl," said he, "would make a delicate titbit to begin dinner with. Just one plump morsel, melting away between the teeth. If he comes within my reach, I'll catch him, and give him to the palace cook to be roasted on a skewer."

The words were hardly out of his mouth, before the purple bird flew away, crying, "Peep, peep, pe--weep," more dolorously than ever.

"That bird," remarked Eurylochus, "knows more than we do about what awaits us at the palace."

"Come on, then," cried his comrades, "and we'll soon know as much as he does."

The party, accordingly, went onward through the green and pleasant wood. Every little while they caught new glimpses of the marble palace, which looked more and more beautiful the nearer they approached it. They soon entered a broad pathway, which seemed to be very neatly kept, and which went winding along, with streaks of sunshine falling across it and specks of light quivering among the deepest shadows that fell from the lofty trees. It was bordered, too, with a great many sweet-smelling flowers, such as the mariners had never seen before. So rich and beautiful they were, that, if the shrubs grew wild here, and were native in the soil, then this island was surely the flower garden of the whole earth; or, if transplanted from some other clime, it must have been from the Happy Islands that lay towards the golden sunset.

"There has been a great deal of pains foolishly wasted on these flowers," observed one of the company; and I tell you what he said, that you may keep in mind what gormandizers they were. "For my part, if I were the owner of the palace, I would bid my gardener cultivate nothing but savory pot herbs to make a stuffing for roast meat, or to flavor a stew with."

" Well said!" cried the others. "But I'll warrant you there's a kitchen garden in the rear of the palace."

At one place they came to a crystal spring, and paused to drink at it for want of liquor which they liked better. Looking into its bosom, they beheld their own faces dimly reflected, but so extravagantly distorted by the gush and motion of the water, that each one of them appeared to be laughing at himself and all his companions. So ridiculous were these images of themselves, indeed, that they did really laugh aloud, and could hardly be grave again as soon as they wished. And after they had drank, they grew still merrier than before.

"It has a twang of the wine cask in it," said one, smacking his lips.

"Make haste!" cried his fellows: "we'll find the wine cask itself at the palace, and that will be better than a hundred crystal fountains."

Then they quickened their pace, and capered for joy at the thought of the savory banquet at which they hoped to be guests. But Eurylochus told them that he felt as if he were walking in a dream.

"If I am really awake," continued he, "then, in my opinion, we are on the point of meeting with some stranger adventure than any that befell us in the cave of Polyphemus, or among the gigantic man-eating Laestrygons, or in the windy palace of King Aeolus, which stands on a brazen-walled island. This kind of dreamy feeling always comes over me before any wonderful occurrence. If you take my advice, you will turn back."

"No, no," answered his comrades, snuffing the air, in which the scent from the palace kitchen was now very perceptible. "We would not turn back, though we were certain that the king of the Laestrygons, as big as a mountain, would sit at the head of the table, and huge Polyphemus, the one-eyed Cyclops, at its foot."

At length they came within full sight of the palace, which proved to be very large and lofty, with a great number of airy pinnacles upon its roof. Though it was midday, and the sun shone brightly over the marble front, yet its snowy whiteness, and its fantastic style of architecture, made it look unreal, like the frost work on a window pane, or like the shapes of castles which one sees among the clouds by moonlight. But, just then, a puff of wind brought down the smoke of the kitchen chimney among them, and caused each man to smell the odor of the dish that he liked best; and, after scenting it, they thought everything else moonshine, and nothing real save this palace, and save the banquet that was evidently ready to be served up in it.

So they hastened their steps towards the portal, but had not got half way across the wide lawn, when a pack of lions, tigers, and wolves came bounding to meet them. The terrified mariners started back, expecting no better fate than to be torn to pieces and devoured. To their surprise and joy, however, these wild beasts merely capered around them, wagging their tails, offering their heads to be stroked and patted, and behaving just like so many well-bred house dogs, when they wish to express their delight at meeting their master, or their master's friends. The biggest lion licked the feet of Eurylochus; and every other lion, and every wolf and tiger, singled out one of his two and twenty followers, whom the beast fondled as if he loved him better than a beef bone.

But, for all that, Eurylochus imagined that he saw something fierce and savage in their eyes; nor would he have been surprised, at any moment, to feel the big lion's terrible claws, or to see each of the tigers make a deadly spring, or each wolf leap at the throat of the man whom he had fondled. Their mildness seemed unreal, and a mere freak; but their savage nature was as true as their teeth and claws.

Nevertheless, the men went safely across the lawn with the wild beasts frisking about them, and doing no manner of harm; although, as they mounted the steps of the palace, you might possibly have heard a low growl, particularly from the wolves; as if they thought it a pity, after all, to let the strangers pass without so much as tasting what they were made of.

Eurylochus and his followers now passed under a lofty portal, and looked through the open doorway into the interior of the palace. The first thing that they saw was a spacious hall, and a fountain in the middle of it, gushing up towards the ceiling out of a marble basin, and falling back into it with a continual plash. The water of this fountain, as it spouted upward, was constantly taking new shapes, not very distinctly, but plainly enough for a nimble fancy to recognize what they were. Now it was the shape of a man in a long robe, the fleecy whiteness of which was made out of the fountain's spray; now it was a lion, or a tiger, or a wolf, or an ass, or, as often as anything else, a hog, wallowing in the marble basin as if it were his sty. It was either magic or some very curious machinery that caused the gushing waterspout to assume all these forms. But, before the strangers had time to look closely at this wonderful sight, their attention was drawn off by a very sweet and agreeable sound. A woman's voice was singing melodiously in another room of the palace, and with her voice was mingled the noise of a loom, at which she was probably seated, weaving a rich texture of cloth, and intertwining the high and low sweetness of her voice into a rich tissue of harmony.

By and by, the song came to an end; and then, all at once, there were several feminine voices, talking airily and cheerfully, with now and then a merry burst of laughter, such as you may always hear when three or four young women sit at work together.

"What a sweet song that was!" exclaimed one of the voyagers.

"Too sweet, indeed," answered Eurylochus, shaking his head. "Yet it was not so sweet as the song of the Sirens, those bird-like damsels who wanted to tempt us on the rocks, so that our vessel might be wrecked, and our bones left whitening along the shore."

"But just listen to the pleasant voices of those maidens, and that buzz of the loom, as the shuttle passes to and fro," said another comrade. "What a domestic, household, home-like sound it is! Ah, before that weary siege of Troy, I used to hear the buzzing loom and the women's voices under my own roof. Shall I never hear them again? nor taste those nice little savory dishes which my dearest wife knew how to serve up?"

"Tush! we shall fare better here," said another. "But how innocently those women are babbling together, without guessing that we overhear them! And mark that richest voice of all, so pleasant and so familiar, but which yet seems to have the authority of a mistress among them. Let us show ourselves at once. What harm can the lady of the palace and her maidens do to mariners and warriors like us?"

"Remember," said Eurylochus, "that it was a young maiden who beguiled three of our friends into the palace of the king of the Laestrygons, who ate up one of them in the twinkling of an eye."

No warning or persuasion, however, had any effect on his companions. They went up to a pair of folding doors at the farther end of the hall, and throwing them wide open, passed into the next room. Eurylochus, meanwhile, had stepped behind a pillar. In the short moment while the folding doors opened and closed again, he caught a glimpse of a very beautiful woman rising from the loom, and coming to meet the poor weather-beaten wanderers, with a hospitable smile, and her hand stretched out in welcome. There were four other young women, who joined their hands and danced merrily forward, making gestures of obeisance to the strangers. They were only less beautiful than the lady who seemed to be their mistress. Yet Eurylochus fancied that one of them had sea-green hair, and that the close-fitting bodice of a second looked like the bark of a tree, and that both the others had something odd in their aspect, although he could not quite determine what it was, in the little while that he had to examine them.

The folding doors swung quickly back, and left him standing behind the pillar, in the solitude of the outer hall. There Eurylochus waited until he was quite weary, and listened eagerly to every sound, but without hearing anything that could help him to guess what had become of his friends. Footsteps, it is true, seemed to be passing and repassing, in other parts of the palace. Then there was a clatter of silver dishes, or golden ones, which made him imagine a rich feast in a splendid banqueting hall. But by and by he heard a tremendous grunting and squealing, and then a sudden scampering, like that of small, hard hoofs over a marble floor, while the voices of the mistress and her four handmaidens were screaming all together, in tones of anger and derision. Eurylochus could not conceive what had happened, unless a drove of swine had broken into the palace, attracted by the smell of the feast. Chancing to cast his eyes at the fountain, he saw that it did not shift its shape, as formerly, nor looked either like a long-robed man, or a lion, a tiger, a wolf, or an ass. It looked like nothing but a hog, which lay wallowing in the marble basin, and filled it from brim to brim.

But we must leave the prudent Eurylochus waiting in the outer hall, and follow his friends into the inner secrecy of the palace. As soon as the beautiful woman saw them, she arose from the loom, as I have told you, and came forward, smiling, and stretching out her hand. She took the hand of the foremost among them, and bade him and the whole party welcome.

"You have been long expected, my good friends," said she. "I and my maidens are well acquainted with you, although you do not appear to recognize us. Look at this piece of tapestry, and judge if your faces must not have been familiar to us."

So the voyagers examined the web of cloth which the beautiful woman had been weaving in her loom; and, to their vast astonishment, they saw their own figures perfectly represented in different colored threads. It was a life-like picture of their recent adventures, showing them in the cave of Polyphemus, and how they had put out his one great moony eye; while in another part of the tapestry they were untying the leathern bags, puffed out with contrary winds; and farther on, they beheld themselves scampering away from the gigantic king of the Laestrygons, who had caught one of them by the leg. Lastly, there they were, sitting on the desolate shore of this very island, hungry and downcast, and looking ruefully at the bare bones of the stag which they devoured yesterday. This was as far as the work had yet proceeded; but when the

    An Old Woman's Tale and other writings

beautiful woman should again sit down at her loom, she would probably make a picture of what had since happened to the strangers, and of what was now going to happen.

"You see," she said, "that I know all about your troubles; and you cannot doubt that I desire to make you happy for as long a time as you may remain with me. For this purpose, my honored guests, I have ordered a banquet to be prepared. Fish, fowl, and flesh, roasted, and in luscious stews, and seasoned, I trust, to all your tastes, are ready to be served up. If your appetites tell you it is dinner time, then come with me to the festal saloon."

At this kind invitation, the hungry mariners were quite overjoyed; and one of them, taking upon himself to be spokesman, assured their hospitable hostess that any hour of the day was dinner time with them, whenever they could get flesh to put in the pot, and fire to boil it with. So the beautiful woman led the way; and the four maidens (one of them had sea-green hair, another a bodice of oak bark, a third sprinkled a shower of water drops from her fingers' ends, and the fourth had some other oddity, which I have forgotten), all these followed behind, and hurried the guests along, until they entered a magnificent saloon. It was built in a perfect oval, and lighted from a crystal dome above. Around the walls were ranged two and twenty thrones, overhung by canopies of crimson and gold, and provided with the softest of cushions, which were tasselled and fringed with gold cord. Each of the strangers was invited to sit down; and there they were, two and twenty storm- beaten mariners, in worn and tattered garb, sitting on two and twenty cushioned and canopied thrones, so rich and gorgeous that the proudest monarch had nothing more splendid in his stateliest hall.

Then you might have seen the guests nodding, winking with one eye, and leaning from one throne to another, to communicate their satisfaction in hoarse whispers.

"Our good hostess has made kings of us all," said one. "Ha! do you smell the feast? I'll engage it will be fit to set before two and twenty kings."

"I hope," said another, "it will be, mainly, good substantial joints, sirloins, spareribs, and hinder quarters, without too many kickshaws. If I thought the good lady would not take it amiss, I should call for a fat slice of fried bacon to begin with."

Ah, the gluttons and gormandizers! You see how it was with them. In the loftiest seats of dignity, on royal thrones, they could think of nothing but their greedy appetite, which was the portion of their nature that they shared with wolves and swine; so that they resembled those vilest of animals far more than they did kings--if, indeed, kings were what they ought to be.

But the beautiful woman now clapped her hands; and immediately there entered a train of two and twenty serving man, bringing dishes of the richest food, all hot from the kitchen fire, and sending up such a steam that it hung like a cloud below the crystal dome of the saloon. An equal number of attendants brought great flagons of wine, of various kinds, some of which sparkled as it was poured out, and went bubbling down the throat; while, of other sorts, the purple liquor was so clear that you could see the wrought figures at the bottom of the goblet. While the servants supplied the two and twenty guests with food and drink, the hostess and her four maidens went from one throne to another, exhorting them to eat their fill, and to quaff wine abundantly, and thus to recompense them- selves, at this one banquet, for the many days when they had gone without a dinner. But whenever the mariners were not looking at them (which was pretty often, as they looked chiefly into the basins and platters), the beautiful woman and her damsels turned aside, and laughed. Even the servants, as they knelt down to present the dishes, might be seen to grin and sneer, while the guests were helping themselves to the offered dainties.

And, once in a while, the strangers seemed to taste something that they did not like.

"Here is an odd kind of spice in this dish," said one. "I can't say it quite suits my palate. Down it goes, however."

"Send a good draught of wine down your throat," said his comrade on the next throne. "That is the stuff to make this sort of cookery relish well. Though I must needs say, the wine has a queer taste too. But the more I drink of it, the better I like the flavor."

Whatever little fault they might find with the dishes, they sat at dinner a prodigiously long while; and it would really have made you ashamed to see how they swilled down the liquor and gobbled up the food. They sat on golden thrones, to be sure; but they behaved like pigs in a sty; and, if they had had their wits about them, they might have guessed that this was the opinion of their beautiful hostess and her maidens. It brings a blush into my face to reckon up, in my own mind, what mountains of meat and pudding, and what gallons of wine, these two and twenty guzzlers and gormandizers ate and drank. They forgot all about their homes, and their wives and children, and all about Ulysses, and everything else, except this banquet, at which they wanted to keep feasting forever. But at length they began to give over, from mere incapacity to hold any more.

"That last bit of fat is too much for me," said one.

"And I have not room for another morsel," said his next neighbor, heaving a sigh. "What a pity! My appetite is as sharp as ever."

In short, they all left off eating, and leaned back on their thrones, with such a stupid and helpless aspect as made them ridiculous to behold. When their hostess saw this, she laughed aloud; so did her four damsels; so did the two and twenty serving men that bore the dishes, and their two and twenty fellows that poured out the wine. And the louder they all laughed, the more stupid and helpless did the two and twenty gormandizers look. Then the beautiful woman took her stand in the middle of the saloon, and stretching out a slender rod (it had been all the while in her hand, although they never noticed it till this moment), she turned it from one guest to another, until each had felt it pointed at himself. Beautiful as her face was, and though there was a smile on it, it looked just as wicked and mischievous as the ugliest serpent that ever was seen; and fat-witted as the voyagers had made themselves, they began to suspect that they had fallen into the power of an evil-minded enchantress.

"Wretches," cried she, "you have abused a lady's hospitality; and in this princely saloon your behavior has been suited to a hog-pen. You are already swine in everything but the human form, which you disgrace, and which I myself should be ashamed to keep a moment longer, were you to share it with me. But it will require only the slightest exercise of magic to make the exterior conform to the hoggish disposition. Assume your proper shapes, gormandizers, and begone to the sty!"

Uttering these last words, she waved her wand; and stamping her foot imperiously, each of the guests was struck aghast at beholding, instead of his comrades in human shape, one and twenty hogs sitting on the same number of golden thrones. Each man (as he still supposed himself to be) essayed to give a cry of surprise, but found that he could merely grunt, and that, in a word, he was just such another beast as his companions. It looked so intolerably absurd to see hogs on cushioned thrones, that they made haste to wallow down upon all fours, like other swine. They tried to groan and beg for mercy, but forthwith emitted the most awful grunting and squealing that ever came out of swinish throats. They would have wrung their hands in despair, but, attempting to do so, grew all the more desperate for seeing themselves squatted on their hams, and pawing the air with their fore trotters. Dear me! what pendulous ears they had! what little red eyes, half buried in fat! and what long snouts, instead of Grecian noses!

But brutes as they certainly were, they yet had enough of human nature in them to be shocked at their own hideousness; and still intending to groan, they uttered a viler grunt and squeal than before. So harsh and ear-piercing it was, that you would have fancied a butcher was sticking his knife into each of their throats, or, at the very least, that somebody was pulling every hog by his funny little twist of a tail.

"Begone to your sty!" cried the enchantress, giving them some smart strokes with her wand; and then she turned to the serving men--"Drive out these swine, and throw down some acorns for them to eat."

The door of the saloon being flung open, the drove of hogs ran in all directions save the right one, in accordance with their hoggish perversity, but were finally driven into the back yard of the palace. It was a sight to bring tears into one's eyes (and I hope none of you will be cruel enough to laugh at it), to see the poor creatures go snuffing along, picking up here a cabbage leaf and there a turnip top, and rooting their noses in the earth for whatever they could find. In their sty, moreover, they behaved more piggishly than the pigs that had been born so; for they bit and snorted at one another, put their feet in the trough, and gobbled up their victuals in a ridiculous hurry; and, when there was nothing more to be had, they made a great pile of themselves among some unclean straw, and fell fast asleep. If they had any human reason left, it was just enough to keep them wondering when they should be slaughtered, and what quality of bacon they should make.

Meantime, as I told you before, Eurylochus had waited, and waited, and waited, in the entrance hall of the palace, without being able to comprehend what had befallen his friends. At last, when the swinish uproar resounded through the palace, and when he saw the image of a hog in the marble basin, he thought it best to hasten back to the vessel, and inform the wise Ulysses of these marvelous occurrences. So he ran as fast as he could down the steps, and never stopped to draw breath till he reached the shore.

"Why do you come alone?" asked King Ulysses, as soon as he saw him. "Where are your two and twenty comrades?"

At these questions, Eurylochus burst into tears.

"Alas!" he cried, "I greatly fear that we shall never see one of their faces again."

Then he told Ulysses all that had happened, as far as he knew it, and added that he suspected the beautiful woman to be a vile enchantress, and the marble palace, magnificent as it looked, to be only a dismal cavern in reality. As for his companions, he could not imagine what had become of them, unless they had been given to the swine to be devoured alive. At this intelligence, all the voyagers were greatly affrighted. But Ulysses lost no time in girding on his sword, and hanging his bow and quiver over his shoulders, and. taking a spear in his right hand. When his followers saw their wise leader making these preparations, they inquired whither he was going, and earnestly besought him not to leave them.

"You are our king," cried they; "and what is more, you are the wisest man in the whole world, and nothing but your wisdom and courage can get us out of this danger. If you desert us, and go to the enchanted palace, you will suffer the same fate as our poor companions, and not a soul of us will ever see our dear Ithaca again."

"As I am your king," answered Ulysses, "and wiser than any of you, it is therefore the more my duty to see what has befallen our comrades, and whether anything can yet be done to rescue them. Wait for me here until tomorrow. If I do not then return, you must hoist sail, and endeavor to find your way

   An Old Woman's Tale and other writings

to our native land. For my part, I am answerable for the fate of these poor mariners, who have stood by my side in battle, and been so often drenched to the skin, along with me, by the same tempestuous surges. I will either bring them back with me, or perish."

Had his followers dared, they would have detained him by force. But King Ulysses frowned sternly on them, and shook his spear, and bade them stop him at their peril. Seeing him so determined, they let him go, and sat down on the sand, as disconsolate a set of people as could be, waiting and praying for his return.

It happened to Ulysses, just as before, that, when he had gone a few steps from the edge of the cliff, the purple bird came fluttering towards him, crying, "Peep, peep, pe--weep!" and using all the art it could to persuade him to go no farther.

"What mean you, little bird?" cried Ulysses. "You are arrayed like a king in purple and gold, and wear a golden crown upon your head. Is it because I too am a king, that you desire so earnestly to speak with me? If you can talk in human language, say what you would have me do."

"Peep!" answered the purple bird, very dolorously. "Peep, peep, pe--we--e!"

Certainly there lay some heavy anguish at the little bird's heart; and it was a sorrowful predicament that he could not, at least, have the consolation of telling what it was. But Ulysses had no time to waste in trying to get at the mystery. He therefore quickened his pace, and had gone a good way along the pleasant wood path, when there met him a young man of very brisk and intelligent aspect, and clad in a rather singular garb. He wore a short cloak and a sort of cap that seemed to be furnished with a pair of wings; and from the lightness of his step, you would have supposed that there might likewise be wings on his feet. To enable him to walk still better (for he was always on one journey or another) he carried a winged staff, around which two serpents were wriggling and twisting. In short, I have said enough to make you guess that it was Quicksilver; and Ulysses (who knew him of old, and had learned a great deal of his wisdom from him) recognized him in a moment.

"Whither are you going in such a hurry, wise Ulysses?" asked Quicksilver. "Do you not know that this island is enchanted? The wicked enchantress (whose name is Circe, the sister of King Aetes) dwells in the marble palace which you see yonder among the trees. By her magic arts she changes every human being into the brute, beast, or fowl whom he happens most to resemble."

"That little bird, which met me at the edge of the cliff," exclaimed Ulysses; "was he a human being once?"

"Yes," answered Quicksilver. "He was once a king, named Picus, and a pretty good sort of a king, too, only rather too proud of his purple robe, and his crown, and the golden chain about his neck; so he was forced to take the shape of a gaudy-feathered bird. The lions, and wolves, and tigers, who will come running to meet you, in front of the palace, were formerly fierce and cruel men, resembling in their disposition the wild beasts whose forms they now rightfully wear."

"And my poor companions," said Ulysses. "Have they undergone a similar change, through the arts of this wicked Circe?"

"You well know what gormandizers they were," replied Quicksilver; and rogue that he was, he could not help laughing at the joke. "So you will not be surprised to hear that they have all taken the shapes of swine! If Circe had never done anything worse, I really should not think her so very much to blame."

"But can I do nothing to help them?" inquired Ulysses.

"It will require all your wisdom," said Quicksilver, "and

a little of my own into the bargain, to keep your royal and sagacious self from being transformed into a fox. But do as I bid you; and the matter may end better than it has begun."

While he was speaking, Quicksilver seemed to be in search of something; he went stooping along the ground, and soon laid his hand on a little plant with a snow-white flower, which he plucked and smelt of. Ulysses had been looking at that very spot only just before; and it appeared to him that the plant had burst into full flower the instant when Quicksilver touched it with his fingers.

"Take this flower, King Ulysses," said he. "Guard it as you do your eyesight; for I can assure you it is exceedingly rare and precious, and you might seek the whole earth over without ever finding another like it. Keep it in your hand, and smell of it frequently after you enter the palace, and while you are talking with the enchantress. Especially when she offers you food, or a draught of wine out of her goblet, be careful to fill your nostrils with the flower's fragrance. Follow these directions, and you may defy her magic arts to change you into a fox."

Quicksilver then gave him some further advice how to behave, and bidding him be bold and prudent, again assured him that, powerful as Circe was, he would have a fair prospect of coming safely out of her enchanted palace. After listening attentively, Ulysses thanked his good friend, and resumed his way. But he had taken only a few steps, when, recollecting some other questions which he wished to ask, he turned round again, and beheld nobody on the spot where Quicksilver had stood; for that winged cap of his, and those winged shoes, with the help of the winged staff, had carried him quickly out of sight.

When Ulysses reached the lawn, in front of the palace, the lions and other savage animals came bounding to meet him, and would have fawned upon him and licked his feet. But the wise king struck at them with his long spear, and sternly bade them begone out of his path; for he knew that they had once been bloodthirsty men, and would now tear him limb from limb, instead of fawning upon him, could they do the mischief that was in their hearts. The wild beasts yelped and glared at him, and stood at a distance, while he ascended the palace steps.

On entering the hall, Ulysses saw the magic fountain in the center of it. The up-gushing water had now again taken the shape of a man in a long, white, fleecy robe, who appeared to be making gestures of welcome. The king likewise heard the noise of the shuttle in the loom and the sweet melody of the beautiful woman's song, and then the pleasant voices of herself and the four maidens talking together, with peals of merry laughter intermixed. But Ulysses did not waste much time in listening to the laughter or the song. He leaned his spear against one of the pillars of the hall, and then, after loosening his sword in the scabbard, stepped boldly forward, and threw the folding doors wide open. The moment she beheld his stately figure standing in the doorway, the beautiful woman rose from the loom, and ran to meet him with a glad smile throwing its sunshine over her face, and both her hands extended.

"Welcome, brave stranger!" cried she. "We were expecting you."

And the nymph with the sea-green hair made a courtesy down to the ground, and likewise bade him welcome; so did her sister with the bodice of oaken bark, and she that sprinkled dew-drops from her fingers' ends, and the fourth one with some oddity which I cannot remember. And Circe, as the beautiful enchantress was called (who had deluded so many persons that she did not doubt of being able to delude Ulysses, not imagining how wise he was), again addressed him:

"Your companions," said she, "have already been received into my palace, and have enjoyed the hospitable treatment to which the propriety of their behavior so well entitles them. If such be your pleasure, you shall first take some refreshment, and then join them in the elegant apartment which they now occupy. See, I and my maidens have been weaving their figures into this piece of tapestry."

She pointed to the web of beautifully-woven cloth in the loom. Circe and the four nymphs must have been very diligently at work since the arrival of the mariners; for a great many yards of tapestry had now been wrought, in addition to what I before described. In this new part, Ulysses saw his two and twenty friends represented as sitting on cushions and canopied thrones, greedily devouring dainties, and quaffing deep draughts of wine. The work had not yet gone any further. O, no, indeed. The enchantress was far too cunning to let Ulysses see the mischief which her magic arts had since brought upon the gormandizers.

"As for yourself, valiant sir," said Circe, "judging by the dignity of your aspect, I take you to be nothing less than a king. Deign to follow me, and you shall be treated as befits your rank."

So Ulysses followed her into the oval saloon, where his two and twenty comrades had devoured the banquet, which ended so disastrously for themselves. But, all this while, he had held the snow-white flower in his hand, and had constantly smelt of it while Circe was speaking; and as he crossed the threshold of the saloon, he took good care to inhale several long and deep snuffs of its fragrance. Instead of two and twenty thrones, which had before been ranged around the wall, there was now only a single throne, in the center of the apartment. But this was surely the most magnificent seat that ever a king or an emperor reposed himself upon, all made of chased gold, studded with precious stones, with a cushion that looked like a soft heap of living roses, and overhung by a canopy of sunlight which Circe knew how to weave into drapery. The enchantress took Ulysses by the hand, and made him sit down upon this dazzling throne. Then, clapping her hands, she summoned the chief butler.

"Bring hither," said she, "the goblet that is set apart for kings to drink out of. And fill it with the same delicious wine which my royal brother, King Aetes, praised so highly, when he last visited me with my fair daughter Medea. That good and amiable child! Were she now here, it would delight her to see me offering this wine to my honored guest."

But Ulysses, while the butler was gone for the wine, held the snow-white flower to his nose.

"Is it a wholesome wine?" he asked.

At this the four maidens tittered; whereupon the enchantress looked round at them, with an aspect of severity.

"It is the wholesomest juice that ever was squeezed out of the grape," said she; "for, instead of disguising a man, as other liquor is apt to do, it brings him to his true self, and shows him as he ought to be."

The chief butler liked nothing better than to see people turned into swine, or making any kind of a beast of themselves; so he made haste to bring the royal goblet, filled with a liquid as bright as gold, and which kept sparkling upward, and throwing a sunny spray over the brim. But, delightfully as the wine looked, it was mingled with the most potent enchantments that Circe knew how to concoct. For every drop of the pure grape juice there were two drops of the pure mischief; and the danger of the thing was, that the mischief made it taste all the better. The mere smell of the bubbles, which effervesced at the brim, was enough to turn a man's beard into pig's bristles, or make a lion's claws grow out of his fingers, or a fox's brush behind him.

"Drink, my noble guest," said Circe, smiling, as she presented him with the goblet. "You will find in this draught a

   An Old Woman's Tale and other writings

solace for all your troubles."

King Ulysses took the goblet with his right hand, while with his left he held the snow-white flower to his nostrils, and drew in so long a breath that his lungs were quite filled with its pure and simple fragrance. Then, drinking off all the wine, he looked the enchantress calmly in the face.

"Wretch," cried Circe, giving him a smart stroke with her wand, "how dare you keep your human shape a moment longer! Take the form of the brute whom you most resemble. If a hog, go join your fellow-swine in the sty; if a lion, a wolf, a tiger, go howl with the wild beasts on the lawn; if a fox, go exercise your craft in stealing poultry. Thou hast quaffed off my wine, and canst be man no longer."

But, such was the virtue of the snow-white flower, instead of wallowing down from his throne in swinish shape, or taking any other brutal form, Ulysses looked even more manly and king-like than before. He gave the magic goblet a toss, and sent it clashing over the marble floor to the farthest end of the saloon. Then, drawing his sword, he seized the enchantress by her beautiful ringlets, and made a gesture as if he meant to strike off her head at one blow.

"Wicked Circe," cried he, in a terrible voice, "this sword shall put an end to thy enchant meets. Thou shalt die, vile wretch, and do no more mischief in the world, by tempting human beings into the vices which make beasts of them."

The tone and countenance of Ulysses were so awful, and his sword gleamed so brightly, and seemed to have so intolerably keen an edge, that Circe was almost killed by the mere fright, without waiting for a blow. The chief butler scrambled out of the saloon, picking up the golden goblet as he went; and the enchantress and the four maidens fell on their knees, wringing their hands, and screaming for mercy.

"Spare me!" cried Circe. "Spare me, royal and wise Ulysses.

For now I know that thou art he of whom Quicksilver forewarned me, the most prudent of mortals, against whom no enchantments can prevail. Thou only couldst have conquered Circe. Spare me, wisest of men. I will show thee true hospitality, and even give myself to be thy slave, and this magnificent palace to be henceforth thy home."

The four nymphs, meanwhile, were making a most piteous ado; and especially the ocean nymph, with the sea-green hair, wept a great deal of salt water, and the fountain nymph, besides scattering dewdrops from her fingers' ends, nearly melted away into tears. But Ulysses would not be pacified until Circe had taken a solemn oath to change back his companions, and as many others as he should direct, from their present forms of beast or bird into their former shapes of men.

"On these conditions," said he, "I consent to spare your life. Otherwise you must die upon the spot."

With a drawn sword hanging over her, the enchantress would readily have consented to do as much good as she had hitherto done mischief, however little she might like such employment. She therefore led Ulysses out of the back entrance of the palace, and showed him the swine in their sty. There were about fifty of these unclean beasts in the whole herd; and though the greater part were hogs by birth and education, there was wonderfully little difference to be seen betwixt them and their new brethren, who had so recently worn the human shape. To speak critically, indeed, the latter rather carried the thing to excess, and seemed to make it a point to wallow in the miriest part of the sty, and otherwise to outdo the original swine in their own natural vocation. When men once turn to brutes, the trifle of man's wit that remains in them adds tenfold to their brutality.

The comrades of Ulysses, however, had not quite lost the remembrance of having formerly stood erect. When he approached the sty, two and twenty enormous swine separated themselves from the herd, and scampered towards him, with such a chorus of horrible squealing as made him clap both hands to his ears. And yet they did not seem to know what they wanted, nor whether they were merely hungry, or miserable from some other cause. It was curious, in the midst of their distress, to observe them thrusting their noses into the mire, in quest of something to eat. The nymph with the bodice of oaken bark (she was the hamadryad of an oak) threw a handful of acorns among them; and the two and twenty hogs scrambled and fought for the prize, as if they had tasted not so much as a noggin of sour milk for a twelvemonth.

"These must certainly be my comrades," said Ulysses. "I recognize their dispositions. They are hardly worth the trouble of changing them into the human form again. Nevertheless, we will have it done, lest their bad example should corrupt the other hogs. Let them take their original shapes, therefore, Dame Circe, if your skill is equal to the task. It will require greater magic, I trow, than it did to make swine of them."

So Circe waved her wand again, and repeated a few magic words, at the sound of which the two and twenty hogs pricked up their pendulous ears. It was a wonder to behold how their snouts grew shorter and shorter, and their mouths (which they seemed to be sorry for, because they could not gobble so expeditiously) smaller and smaller, and how one and another began to stand upon his hind legs, and scratch his nose with his fore trotters. At first the spectators hardly knew whether to call them hogs or men, but by and by came to the conclusion that they rather resembled the latter. Finally, there stood the twenty-two comrades of Ulysses, looking pretty much the same as when they left the vessel.

You must not imagine, however, that the swinish quality had entirely gone out of them. When once it fastens itself into a person's character, it is very difficult getting rid of it. This was proved by the hamadryad, who, being exceedingly fond of mischief, threw another handful of acorns before the twenty-two newly-restored people; whereupon down they wallowed in a moment, and gobbled them up in a very shameful way. Then, recollecting themselves, they scrambled to their feet, and looked more than commonly foolish.

"Thanks, noble Ulysses!" they cried. "From brute beasts you have restored us to the condition of men again."

"Do not put yourselves to the trouble of thanking me," said the wise king. "I fear I have done but little for you."

To say the truth, there was a suspicious kind of a grunt in their voices, and, for a long time afterwards, they spoke gruffly, and were apt to set up a squeal.

"It must depend on your own future behavior," added Ulysses, "whether you do not find your way back to the sty."

At this moment, the note of a bird sounded from the branch of a neighboring tree.

"Peep, peep, pe--wee--e!"

It was the purple bird, who, all this while, had been sitting over their heads, watching what was going forward, and hoping that Ulysses would remember how he had done his utmost to keep him and his followers out of harm's way. Ulysses ordered Circe instantly to make a king of this good little fowl, and leave him exactly as she found him. Hardly were the words spoken, and before the bird had time to utter another "pe--weep," King Picus leaped down from the bough of a tree, as majestic a sovereign as any in the world, dressed in a long purple robe and gorgeous yellow stockings, with a splendidly wrought collar about his neck, and a golden crown upon his head. He and King Ulysses exchanged with one another the courtesies which belong to their elevated rank. But from that time forth, King Picus was no longer proud of his crown and his trappings of royalty, nor of the fact of his being a king; he felt himself merely the upper servant of his people, and that it must be his life-long labor to make them better and happier.

As for the lions, tigers, and wolves (though Circe would have restored them to their former shapes at his slightest word), Ulysses thought it advisable that they should remain as they now were, and thus give warning of their cruel dispositions, instead of going about under the guise of men, and pretending to human sympathies, while their hearts had the blood- thirstiness of wild beasts. So he let them howl as much as they liked, but never troubled his head about them. And, when everything was settled according to his pleasure, he sent to summon the remainder of his comrades, whom he had left at the sea-shore. These being arrived, with the prudent Eurylochus at their head, they all made themselves comfortable in Circe's enchanted palace, until quite rested and refreshed from the toils and hardships of their voyage.

David Swan

We can be but partially acquainted even with the events which actually influence our course through life, and our final destiny. There are innumerable other events--if such they may be called--which come close upon us, yet pass away without actual results, or even betraying their near approach, by the reflection of any light or shadow across our minds. Could we know all the vicissitudes of our fortunes, life would be too full of hope and fear, exultation or disappointment, to afford us a single hour of true serenity. This idea may be illustrated by a page from the secret history of David Swan.

We have nothing to do with David until we find him, at the age of twenty, on the high road from his native place to the city of Boston, where his uncle, a small dealer in the grocery line, was to take him behind the counter. Be it enough to say that he was a native of New Hampshire, born of respectable parents, and had received an ordinary school education, with a classic finish by a year at Gilmanton Academy. After journeying on foot from sunrise till nearly noon of a summer's day, his weariness and the increasing heat determined him to sit down in the first convenient shade, and await the coming up of the stage-coach. As if planted on purpose for him, there soon appeared a little tuft of maples, with a delightful recess in the midst, and such a fresh bubbling spring that it seemed never to have sparkled for any wayfarer but David Swan. Virgin or not, he kissed it with his thirsty lips, and then flung himself along the brink, pillowing his head upon some shirts and a pair of pantaloons, tied up in a striped cotton handkerchief. The sunbeams could not reach him; the dust did not yet rise from the road after the heavy rain of yesterday; and his grassy lair suited the young man better than a bed of down. The spring murmured drowsily beside him; the branches waved dreamily across the blue sky overhead; and a deep sleep, perchance hiding dreams within its depths, fell upon David Swan. But we are to relate events which he did not dream of.

While he lay sound asleep in the shade, other people were wide awake, and passed to and fro, afoot, on horseback, and in all sorts of vehicles, along the sunny road by his bedchamber. Some looked neither to the right hand nor the left, and knew not that he was there; some merely glanced that way, without admitting the slumberer among their busy thoughts; some laughed to see how soundly he slept; and several, whose hearts were brimming full of scorn, ejected their venomous superfluity on David Swan. A middle-aged widow, when nobody else was near, thrust her head a little way into the recess, and vowed that the young fellow looked charming in his sleep. A temperance lecturer saw him, and wrought poor David into the texture of his evening's discourse, as an awful instance of dead drunkenness by the roadside. But censure, praise, merriment, scorn, and indifference were all one, or rather all nothing, to David Swan.

He had slept only a few moments when a brown carriage, drawn by a handsome pair of horses, bowled easily along, and was brought to a standstill nearly in front of David's resting-place. A linchpin had fallen out, and permitted one of the wheels to slide off. The damage was slight, and occasioned merely a momentary alarm to an elderly merchant and his wife, who were returning to Boston in the carriage. While the coachman and a servant were replacing the wheel, the lady and gentleman sheltered themselves beneath the maple-trees, and there espied the bubbling fountain, and David Swan asleep beside it. Impressed with the awe which the humblest sleeped usually sheds around him, the merchant trod as lightly as the gout would allow; and his spouse took good heed not to rustle her silk gown, lest David should start up all of a sudden.

"How soundly he sleeps!" whispered the old gentleman. "From what a depth he draws that easy breath! Such sleep as that, brought on without an opiate, would be worth more to me than half my income; for it would suppose health and an untroubled mind."

"And youth, besides," said the lady. "Healthy and quiet age does not sleep thus. Our slumber is no more like his than our wakefulness."

The longer they looked the more did this elderly couple feel interested in the unknown youth, to whom the wayside and the maple shade were as a secret chamber, with the rich gloom of damask curtains brooding over him. Perceiving that a stray sunbeam glimmered down upon his face, the lady contrived to twist a branch aside, so as to intercept it. And having done this little act of kindness, she began to feel like a mother to him.

"Providence seems to have laid him here," whispered she to her husband, "and to have brought us hither to find him, after our disappointment in our cousin's son. Methinks I can see a likeness to our departed Henry. Shall we waken him?"

"To what purpose?" said the merchant, hesitating. "We know nothing of the youth's character."

"That open countenance!" replied his wife, in the same hushed voice, yet earnestly. "This innocent sleep!"

While these whispers were passing, the sleeper's heart did not throb, nor his breath become agitated, nor his features betray the least token of interest. Yet Fortune was bending over him, just ready to let fall a burden of gold. The old merchant had lost his only son, and had no heir to his wealth except a distant relative, with whose conduct he was dissatisfied. In such cases, people sometimes do stranger things than to act the magician, and awaken a young man to splendor who fell asleep in poverty.

  An Old Woman's Tale and other writings

"Shall we not waken him?" repeated the lady persuasively.

"The coach is ready, sir," said the servant, behind.

The old couple started, reddened, and hurried away, mutually wondering that they should ever have dreamed of doing anything so very ridiculous. The merchant threw himself back in the carriage, and occupied his mind with the plan of a magnificent asylum for unfortunate men of business. Meanwhile, David Swan enjoyed his nap.

The carriage could not have gone above a mile or two, when a pretty young girl came along, with a tripping pace, which showed precisely how her little heart was dancing in her bosom. Perhaps it was this merry kind of motion that caused--is there any harm in saying it?--her garter to slip its knot. Conscious that the silken girth--if silk it were--was relaxing its hold, she turned aside into the shelter of the maple-trees, and there found a young man asleep by the spring! Blushing as red as any rose that she should have intruded into a gentleman's bedchamber, and for such a purpose, too, she was about to make her escape on tiptoe. But there was peril near the sleeper. A monster of a bee had been wandering overhead--buzz, buzz, buzz--now among the leaves, now flashing through the strips of sunshine, and now lost in the dark shade, till finally he appeared to be settling on the eyelid of David Swan. The sting of a bee is sometimes deadly. As free hearted as she was innocent, the girl attacked the intruder with her handkerchief, brushed him soundly, and drove him from beneath the mapleshade. How sweet a picture! This good deed accomplished, with quickened breath, and a deeper blush, she stole a glance at the youthful stranger for whom she had been battling with a dragon in the air.

"He is handsome!" thought she, and blushed redder yet.

How could it be that no dream of bliss grew so strong within him, that, shattered by its very strength, it should part asunder, and allow him to perceive the girl among its phantoms? Why, at least, did no smile of welcome brighten upon his face? She was come, the maid whose soul, according to the old and beautiful idea, had been severed from his own, and whom, in all his vague but passionate desires, he yearned to meet. Her, only, could he love with a perfect love; him, only, could she receive into the depths of her heart; and now her image was faintly blushing in the fountain, by his side; should it pass away, its happy lustre would never gleam upon his life again.

"How sound he sleeps!" murmured the girl.

She departed, but did not trip along the road so lightly as when she came.

Now, this girl's father was a thriving country merchant in the neighborhood, and happened, at that identical time, to be looking out for just such a young man as David Swan. Had David formed a wayside acquaintance with the daughter, he would have become the father's clerk, and all else in natural succession. So here, again, had good fortune--the best of fortunes--stolen so near that her garments brushed against him; and he knew nothing of the matter.

The girl was hardly out of sight when two men turned aside beneath the maple shade. Both had dark faces, set off by cloth caps, which were drawn down aslant over their brows. Their dresses were shabby, yet had a certain smartness. These were a couple of rascals who got their living by whatever the devil sent them, and now, in the interim of other business, had staked the joint profits of their next piece of villany on a game of cards, which was to have been decided here under the trees. But, finding David asleep by the spring, one of the rogues whispered to his fellow,"Hist!--Do you see that bundle under his head?"

The other villain nodded, winked, and leered.

"I'll bet you a horn of brandy," said the first, "that the

chap has either a pocket-book, or a snug little hoard of small change, stowed away amongst his shirts. And if not there, we shall find it in his pantaloons pocket."

"But how if he wakes?" said the other.

His companion thrust aside his waistcoat, pointed to the handle of a dirk, and nodded.

"So be it!" muttered the second villain.

They approached the unconscious David, and, while one pointed the dagger towards his heart, the other began to search the bundle beneath his head. Their two faces, grim, wrinkled, and ghastly with guilt and fear, bent over their victim, looking horrible enough to be mistaken for fiends, should he suddenly awake. Nay, had the villains glanced aside into the spring, even they would hardly have known themselves as reflected there. But David Swan had never worn a more tranquil aspect, even when asleep on his mother's breast.

"I must take away the bundle," whispered one.

"If he stirs, I'll strike," muttered the other.

But, at this moment, a dog scenting along the ground, came in beneath the maple-trees, and gazed alternately at each of these wicked men, and then at the quiet sleeper. He then lapped out of the fountain.

"Pshaw!" said one villain. "We can do nothing now. The dog's master must be close behind."

"Let's take a drink and be off," said the other

The man with the dagger thrust back the weapon into his bosom, and drew forth a pocket pistol, but not of that kind which kills by a single discharge. It was a flask of liquor, with a block-tin tumbler screwed upon the mouth. Each drank a comfortable dram, and left the spot, with so many jests, and such laughter at their unaccomplished wickedness, that they might be said to have gone on their way rejoicing. In a few hours they had forgotten the whole affair, nor once imagined that the recording angel had written down the crime of murder against their souls, in letters as durable as eternity. As for David Swan, he still slept quietly, neither conscious of the shadow of death when it hung over him, nor of the glow of renewed life when that shadow was withdrawn.

He slept, but no longer so quietly as at first. An hour's repose had snatched, from his elastic frame, the weariness with which many hours of toil had burdened it. Now he stirred--now, moved his lips, without a sound--now, talked, in an inward tone, to the noonday spectres of his dream. But a noise of wheels came rattling louder and louder along the road, until it dashed through the dispersing mist of David's slumber-and there was the stage-coach. He started up with all his ideas about him.

"Halloo, driver!--Take a passenger?" shouted he.

"Room on top!" answered the driver.

Up mounted David, and bowled away merrily towards Boston, without so much as a parting glance at that fountain of dreamlike vicissitude. He knew not that a phantom of Wealth had thrown a golden hue upon its waters--nor that one of Love had sighed softly to their murmur--nor that one of Death had threatened to crimson them with his blood--all, in the brief hour since he lay down to sleep. Sleeping or waking, we hear not the airy footsteps of the strange things that almost happen. Does it not argue a superintending Providence that, while viewless and unexpected events thrust themselves continually athwart our path, there should still be regularity enough in mortal life to render foresight even partially available?

Dr. Heidegger's Experiment

That very singular man, old Doctor Heidegger, once invited four venerable friends to meet him in his study. There were three white-bearded gentlemen, Mr. Medbourne, Colonel Killigrew, and Mr. Gascoigne, and a withered gentlewoman whose name was the Widow Wycherley. They were all melancholy old creatures, who had been unfortunate in life, and whose greatest misfortune it was that they were not long ago in their graves. Mr. Medbourne, in the vigor of his age, had been a prosperous merchant, but had lost his all by a frantic speculation, and was no little better than a mendicant. Colonel Killigrew had wasted his best years, and his health and substance, in the pursuit of sinful pleasures, which had given birth to a brood of pains, such as the gout and divers other torments of soul and body. Mr. Gascoigne was a ruined politician, a man of evil fame, or at least had been so, till time had buried him from the knowledge of the present generation, and made him obscure instead of infamous. As for the Widow Wycherley, tradition tells us that she was a great beauty in her day; but, for a long while past, she had lived in deep seclusion, on account of certain scandalous stories which had prejudiced the gentry of the town against her. It is a circumstance worth mentioning that each of these three old gentlemen, Mr. Medbourne, Colonel Killigrew, and Mr. Gascoigne, were early lovers of the Widow Wycherley, and had once been on the point of cutting each other's throats for her sake. And, before proceeding further, I will merely hint that Doctor Heidegger and all his four guests were sometimes thought to be a little beside themselves; as is not unfrequently the case with old people, when worried either by present troubles or woful recollections.

"My dear friends," said Doctor Heidegger, motioning

them to be seated, "I am desirous of your assistance in one of those little experiments with which I amuse myself here in my study."

If all stories were true, Doctor Heidegger's study must have been a very curious place. It was a dim, old-fashioned chamber, festooned with cobwebs and besprinkled with antique dust. Around the walls stood several oaken bookcases, the lower shelves of which were filled with rows of gigantic folios and black-letter quartos, and the upper with little parchment-covered duodecimos. Over the central bookcase was a bronze bust of Hippocrates, with which, according to some authorities, Doctor Heidegger was accustomed to hold consultations in all difficult cases of his practice. In the obscurest corner of the room stood a tall and narrow oaken closet, with its door ajar, within which doubtfully appeared a skeleton. Between two of the bookcases hung a looking-glass, presenting its high and dusty plate within a tarnished gilt frame. Among many wonderful stories related of this mirror, it was fabled that the spirits of all the doctor's deceased patients dwelt within its verge, and would stare him in the face whenever he looked thitherward. The opposite side of the chamber was ornamented with the full-length portrait of a young lady, arrayed in the faded magnificence of silk, satin, and brocade, and with a visage as faded as her dress. Above half a century ago Doctor Heidegger had been on the point of marriage with this young lady; but, being affected with some slight disorder, she had swallowed one of her lover's prescriptions, and died on the bridal evening. The greatest curiosity of the study remains to be mentioned; it was a ponderous folio volume, bound in black leather, with massive silver clasps. There were no letters on the back, and nobody could tell the title of the book. But it was well known to be a book of magic; and once, when a chambermaid had lifted it, merely to brush away the dust, the skeleton had rattled in its closet, the picture of the young lady had stepped one foot upon the floor, and several ghastly faces

                                       An Old Woman's Tale and other writings

had peeped forth from the mirror; while the brazen head of Hippocrates frowned, and said: "Forbear!"

Such was Doctor Heidegger's study. On the summer afternoon of our tale a small round table, as black as ebony, stood in the centre of the room, sustaining a cut-glass vase of beautiful form and workmanship. The sunshine came through the window, between the heavy festoons of two faded damask curtains, and fell directly across this vase; so that a mild splendor was reflected from it on the ashen visages of the five old people who sat around. Four champagne glasses were also on the table.

"My dear old friends," repeated Doctor Heidegger, "may I reckon on your aid in performing an exceedingly curious experiment?"

Now Doctor Heidegger was a very strange old gentleman, whose eccentricity had become the nucleus for a thousand fantastic stories. Some of these fables, to my shame be it spoken, might possibly be traced back to mine own veracious self; and if any passages of the present tale should startle the reader's faith, I must be content to bear the stigma of a fiction-monger.

When the doctor's four guests heard him talk of his proposed experiment, they anticipated nothing more wonderful than the murder of a mouse in an air-pump or the examination of a cobweb by the microscope, or some similiar nonsense, with which he was constantly in the habit of pestering his intimates. But without waiting for a reply, Doctor Heidegger hobbled across the chamber, and returned with the same ponderous folio, bound in black leather, which common report affirmed to be a book of magic. Undoing the silver clasps, he opened the volume, and took from among its black-letter pages a rose, or what was once a rose, though now the green leaves and crimson petals had assumed one brownish hue, and the ancient flower seemed ready to crumble to dust in the doctor's hands.

"This rose," said Doctor Heidegger, with a sigh, "this same withered and crumbling flower, blossomed five and fifty years ago. It was given me by Sylvia Ward, whose portrait hangs yonder, and I meant to wear it in my bosom at our wedding. Five and fifty years it has been treasured between the leaves of this old volume. Now, would you deem it possible that this rose of half a century could ever bloom again?"

"Nonsense!" said the Widow Wycherley, with a peevish toss of her head. "You might as well ask whether an old woman's wrinkled face could ever bloom again."

"See!" answered Doctor Heidegger.

He uncovered the vase, and threw the faded rose into the water which it contained. At first, it lay lightly on the surface of the fluid, appearing to imbibe none of its moisture. Soon, however, a singular change began to be visible. The crushed and dried petals stirred, and assumed a deepening tinge of crimson, as if the flower were reviving from a death-like slumber; the slender stalk and twigs of foliage became green; and there was the rose of half a century, looking as fresh as when Sylvia Ward had first given it to her lover. It was scarcely full blown; for some of its delicate red leaves curled modestly around its moist bosom, within which two or three dewdrops were sparkling.

"That is certainly a very pretty deception," said the doctor's friends; careless, however, for they had witnessed greater miracles at a conjurer's show; "pray how was it effected?"

"Did you ever hear of the 'Fountain of Youth,'" asked Doctor Heidegger, "which Ponce de Leon, the Spanish adventurer, went in search of, two or three centuries ago?"

"But did Ponce de Leon ever find it?" said the Widow Wycherley.

"No," answered Doctor Heidegger, "for he never sought it in the right place. The famous Fountain of Youth, if I

 An Old Woman's Tale and other writings

am rightly informed, is situated in the southern part of the Floridian peninsula, not far from Lake Macaco. Its source is overshadowed by several magnolias, which, though numberless centuries old, have been kept as fresh as violets, by the virtues of this wonderful water. An acquaintance of mine, knowing my curiosity in such matters, has sent me what you see in the vase."

"Ahem!" said Colonel Killigrew, who believed not a word of the doctor's story; "and what may be the effect of this fluid on the human frame?"

"You shall judge for yourself, my dear Colonel," replied Doctor Heidegger; "and all of you, my respected friends, are welcome to so much of this admirable fluid as may restore to you the bloom of youth. For my own part, having had much trouble in growing old, I am in no hurry to grow young again. With your permission, therefore, I will merely watch the progress of the experiment."

While he spoke, Doctor Heidegger had been filling the four champagne glasses with the water of the Fountain of Youth. It was apparently impregnated with an effervescent gas; for little bubbles were continually ascending from the depths of the glasses, and bursting in silvery spray at the surface. As the liquor diffused a pleasant perfume, the old people doubted now that it possessed cordial and comfortable properties; and though utter sceptics as to its rejuvenescent power, they were inclined to swallow it at once. But Doctor Heidegger besought them to stay a moment.

"Before you drink, my respectable old friends," said he, "it would be well that, with the experience of a lifetime to direct you, you should draw up a few general rules for your guidance, in passing a second time through the perils of youth. Think what a sin and shame it would be if, with your peculiar advantages, you should not become patterns of virtue and wisdom to all the young people of the age!"

The doctor's four venerable friends made him no answer, except by a feeble and tremulous laugh; so very ridiculous was the idea that, knowing how closely repentance treads behind the steps of error, they should ever go astray again.

"Drink, then," said the doctor, bowing: "I rejoice that I have so well selected the subjects of my experiment."

With palsied hands they raised the glasses to their lips. The liquor, if it really possessed such virtues as Doctor Heidegger imputed to it, could not have been bestowed on four human beings who needed it more wofully. They looked as if they had never known what youth or pleasure was, but had been the offspring of nature's dotage, and always the gray, decrepit, sapless, miserable creatures, who now sat stooping round the doctor's table, without life enough in their souls or bodies to be animated even by the prospect of growing young again. They drank off the water, and replaced their glasses on the table.

Assuredly there was an almost immediate improvement in the aspect of the party, not unlike what might have been produced by a glass of generous wine, together with a sudden glow of cheerful sunshine, brightening over all their visages at once. There was a healthful suffusion on their cheeks, instead of the ashen hue that had made them look so corpselike. They gazed at one another, and fancied that some magic power had really begun to smooth away the deep and sad inscriptions which Father Time had been so long engraving on their brows. The Widow Wycherley adjusted her cap, for she felt almost like a woman again.

"Give us more of this wondrous water!" cried they, eagerly. "We are younger--but we are still too old! Quick--give us more!"

"Patience! patience!" quoth Doctor Heidegger, who sat watching the experiment with philosophic coolness. "You have been a long time growing old. Surely you might be content to grow young in half an hour! But the water is at your service."

Again he filled their glasses with the liquor of youth, enough of which still remained in the vase to turn half the old people in the city to the age of their own grandchildren. While the bubbles were yet sparkling on the brim, the doctor's four guests snatched their glasses from the table, and swallowed the contents at a single gulp. Was it delusion? Even while the draught was passing down their throats it seemed to have wrought a change on their whole systems. Their eyes grew clear and bright; a dark shade deepened among their silvery locks; they sat round the table, three gentlemen of middle age, and a woman hardly beyond her buxom prime.

"My dear widow, you are charming!" cried Colonel Killigrew, whose eyes had been fixed upon her face, while the shadows of age were flitting from it like darkness from the crimson daybreak.

The fair widow knew of old that Colonel Killigrew's compliments were not always measured by sober truth; so she started up and ran to the mirror, still dreading that the ugly visage of an old woman would meet her gaze. Meanwhile the three gentlemen behaved in such a manner as proved that the water of the Fountain of Youth possessed some intoxicating qualities, unless, indeed, their exhilaration of spirits were merely a lightsome dizziness, caused by the sudden removal of the weight of years. Mr. Gascoigne's mind seemed to run on political topics, but whether relating to the past, present, or future could not easily be determined, since the same ideas and phrases have been in vogue these fifty years. Now he rattled forth full-throated sentences about patriotism, national glory, and the people's rights; now he muttered some perilous stuff or other, in a sly and doubtful whisper, so cautiously that even his own conscience could scarcely catch the secret; and now, again, he spoke in measured accents and a deeply deferential tone, as if a royal ear were listening to his well-turned periods. Colonel Killigrew all this time had been trolling forth a jolly battle-song, and ringing his glass toward the buxom figure of the Widow Wycherley. On the other side of the table Mr. Medbourne was involved in a calculation of dollars and cents, with which was strangely intermingled a project for supplying the East Indies with ice, by harnessing a team of whales to the polar icebergs.

As for the Widow Wycherley, she stood before the mirror, courtesying and simpering to her own image, and greeting it as the friend whom she loved better than all the world beside. She thrust her face close to the glass to see whether some long-remembered wrinkle or crow's-foot had indeed vanished. She examined whether the snow had so entirely melted from her hair that the venerable cap could be safely thrown aside. At last, turning briskly away, she came with a sort of dancing step to the table.

"My dear old doctor," cried she, "pray favor me with another glass!"

"Certainly, my dear madam, certainly!" replied the complaisant doctor. "See! I have already filled the glasses."

There, in fact, stood the four glasses, brimful of this wonderful water, the delicate spray of which, as it effervesced from the surface, resembled the tremulous glitter of diamonds. It was now so nearly sunset that the chamber had grown duskier than ever; but a mild and moon-like splendor gleamed from within the vase, and rested alike on the four guests, and on the doctor's venerable figure. He sat in a high-backed, elaborately carved oaken chair, with a gray dignity of aspect that might have well befitted that very Father Time, whose power had never been disputed, save by this fortunate company. Even while quaffing the third draught of the Fountain of Youth, they were almost awed by the expression of his mysterious visage.

But the next moment the exhilarating gush of young life

                    An Old Woman's Tale and other writings

shot through their veins. They were now in the happy prime of youth. Age, with its miserable train of cares, and sorrows, and diseases, was remembered only as the trouble of a dream, from which they had joyously awoke. The fresh gloss of the soul, so early lost, and without which the world's successive scenes had been but a gallery of faded pictures, again threw its enchantment over all their prospects. They felt like new-created beings in a new-created universe.

"We are young! We are young!" they cried, exultingly.

Youth, like the extremity of age, had effaced the strongly marked characteristics of middle life, and mutually assimilated them all. They were a group of merry youngsters, almost maddened with the exuberant frolicsomeness of their years. The most singular effect of their gayety was an impulse to mock the infirmity and decrepitude of which they had so lately been the victims. They laughed loudly at their old-fashioned attire--the wide-skirted coats and flapped waistcoats of the young men, and the ancient cap and gown of the blooming girl. One limped across the floor like a gouty grandfather; one set a pair of spectacles astride of his nose, and pretended to pore over the black-letter pages of the book of magic; a third seated himself in an arm-chair, and strove to imitate the venerable dignity of Doctor Heidegger. Then all shouted mirthfully, and leaped about the room. The Widow Wycherley--if so fresh a damsel could be called a widow--tripped up to the doctor's chair with a mischievous merriment in her rosy face.

"Doctor, you dear old soul," cried she, "get up and dance with me!" And then the four young people laughed louder than ever, to think what a queer figure the poor old doctor would cut.

"Pray excuse me," answered the doctor, quietly. "I am old and rheumatic, and my dancing days were over long ago. But either of these gay young gentlemen will be glad of so pretty a partner."

"Dance with me, Clara!" cried Colonel Killigrew.

"She promised me her hand fifty years ago!" exclaimed Mr. Medbourne.

They all gathered round her. One caught both her hands in his passionate grasp--another threw his arm about her waist--the third buried his hand among the curls that clustered beneath the widow's cap. Blushing, panting, struggling, chiding, laughing, her warm breath fanning each of their faces by turns, she strove to disengage herself, yet still remained in their triple embrace. Never was there a livelier picture of youthful rivalship, with bewitching beauty for the prize. Yet, by a strange deception, owing to the duskiness of the chamber and the antique dresses which they still wore, the tall mirror is said to have reflected the figures of the three old, gray, withered grand-sires, ridiculously contending for the skinny ugliness of a shrivelled grandam.

But they were young: their burning passions proved them so. Inflamed to madness by the coquetry of the girl-widow, who neither granted nor quite withheld her favors, the three rivals began to interchange threatening glances. Still keeping hold of the fair prize, they grappled fiercely at one another's throats. As they struggled to and fro, the table was overturned, and the vase dashed into a thousand fragments. The precious Water of Youth flowed in a bright stream across the floor, moistening the wings of a butterfly, which, grown old in the decline of summer, had alighted there to die. The insect fluttered lightly through the chamber, and settled on the snowy head of Doctor Heidegger.

"Come, come, gentlemen!--come, Madame Wycherley!" exclaimed the doctor, "I really must protest against this riot."

They stood still and shivered; for it seemed as if gray Time were calling them back from their sunny youth, far down into the chill and darksome vale of years. They looked at old Doctor Heidegger, who sat in his carved arm-chair, holding the rose of half a century which he had rescued from among the fragments of the shattered vase. At the motion of his hand the rioters resumed their seats, the more readily because their violent exertions had wearied them, youthful though they were.

"My poor Sylvia's rose!" ejaculated Doctor Heidegger, holding it in the light of the sunset clouds; "it appears to be fading again."

And so it was. Even while the party were looking at it the flower continued to shrivel up, till it became as dry and fragile as when the doctor had first thrown it into the vase. He shook off the few drops of moisture which clung to its petals.

"I love it as well thus as in its dewy freshness," observed he, pressing the withered rose to his withered lips. While he spoke, the butterfly fluttered down from the doctor's snowy head, and fell upon the floor.

His guests shivered again. A strange dullness, whether of the body or spirit they could not tell, was creeping gradually over them all. They gazed at one another, and fancied that each fleeting moment snatched away a charm, and left a deepening furrow where none had been before. Was it an illusion? Had the changes of a lifetime been crowded into so brief a space, and were they now four aged people, sitting with their old friend, Doctor Heidegger?

"Are we grown old again so soon?" cried they, dolefully.

In truth, they had. The Water of Youth possessed merely a virtue more transient than that of wine. The delirium which it created had effervesced away. Yes, they were old again! With a shuddering impulse, that showed her a woman still, the widow clasped her skinny hands over her face, and wished that the coffin lid were over it, since it could be no longer beautiful.

"Yes, friends, ye are old again," said Doctor Heidegger;

"and lo! the Water of Youth is all lavished on the ground. Well, I bemoan it not; for if the fountain gushed at my doorstep, I would not stoop to bathe my lips in it--no, though its delirium were for years instead of moments. Such is the lesson ye have taught me!"

But the doctor's four friends had taught no such lesson to themselves. They resolved forthwith to make a pilgrimage to Florida, and quaff at morning, noon, and night from the Fountain of Youth.

An Old Woman's Tale and other writings

Drowne's Wooden Image

One sunshiny morning, in the good old times of the town of Boston, a young carver in wood, well known by the name of Drowne, stood contemplating a large oaken log, which it was his purpose to convert into the figure-head of a vessel. And while he discussed within his own mind what sort of shape or similitude it were well to bestow upon this excellent piece of timber, there came into Drowne's workshop a certain Captain Hunnewell, owner and commander of the good brig called the Cynosure, which had just returned from her first voyage to Fayal.

"Ah! that will do, Drowne, that will do!" cried the jolly captain, tapping the log with his rattan. "I bespeak this very piece of oak for the figure-head of the Cynosure. She has shown herself the sweetest craft that ever floated, and I mean to decorate her prow with the handsomest image that the skill of man can cut out of timber. And, Drowne, you are the fellow to execute it."

"You give me more credit than I deserve, Captain Hunnewell," said the carver, modestly, yet as one conscious of eminence in his art. "But, for the sake of the good brig, I stand ready to do my best. And which of these designs do you prefer? Here,"--pointing to a staring, half-length figure, in a white wig and scarlet coat,--"here is an excellent model, the likeness of our gracious king. Here is the valiant Admiral Vernon. Or, if you prefer a female figure, what say you to Britannia with the trident?"

"All very fine, Drowne; all very fine," answered the mariner. "But as nothing like the brig ever swam the ocean, so I am determined she shall have such a figure-head as old Neptune never saw in his life. And what is more, as there is a secret in the matter, you must pledge your credit not to betray it."

"Certainly," said Drowne, marvelling, however, what possible mystery there could be in reference to an affair so open, of necessity, to the inspection of all the world as the figure-head of a vessel. "You may depend, captain, on my being as secret as the nature of the case will permit."

Captain Hunnewell then took Drowne by the button, and communicated his wishes in so low a tone that it would be unmannerly to repeat what was evidently intended for the carver's private ear. We shall, therefore, take the opportunity to give the reader a few desirable particulars about Drowne himself.

He was the first American who is known to have attempted--in a very humble line, it is true--that art in which we can now reckon so many names already distinguished, or rising to distinction. From his earliest boyhood he had exhibited a knack--for it would be too proud a word to call it genius--a knack, therefore, for the imitation of the human figure in whatever material came most readily to hand. The snows of a New England winter had often supplied him with a species of marble as dazzlingly white, at least, as the Parian or the Carrara, and if less durable, yet sufficiently so to correspond with any claims to permanent existence possessed by the boy's frozen statues. Yet they won admiration from maturer judges than his school-fellows, and were indeed, remarkably clever, though destitute of the native warmth that might have made the snow melt beneath his hand. As he advanced in life, the young man adopted pine and oak as eligible materials for the display of his skill, which now began to bring him a return of solid silver as well as the empty praise that had been an apt reward enough for his productions of evanescent snow. He became noted for carving ornamental pump heads, and wooden urns for gate posts, and decorations, more grotesque than fanciful, for mantelpieces. No apothecary would have deemed himself in the way of obtaining custom without setting up a gilded mortar, if not a head of Galen or Hippocrates, from the skilful hand of Drowne.

But the great scope of his business lay in the manufacture of figure-heads for vessels. Whether it were the monarch himself, or some famous British admiral or general, or the governor of the province, or perchance the favorite daughter of the ship-owner, there the image stood above the prow, decked out in gorgeous colors, magnificently gilded, and staring the whole world out of countenance, as if from an innate consciousness of its own superiority. These specimens of native sculpture had crossed the sea in all directions, and been not ignobly noticed among the crowded shipping of the Thames and wherever else the hardy mariners of New England had pushed their adventures. It must be confessed that a family likeness pervaded these respectable progeny of Drowne's skill; that the benign countenance of the king resembled those of his subjects, and that Miss Peggy Hobart, the merchant's daughter, bore a remarkable similitude to Britannia, Victory, and other ladies of the allegoric sisterhood; and, finally, that they all had a kind of wooden aspect which proved an intimate relationship with the unshaped blocks of timber in the carver's workshop. But at least there was no inconsiderable skill of hand, nor a deficiency of any attribute to render them really works of art, except that deep quality, be it of soul or intellect, which bestows life upon the lifeless and warmth upon the cold, and which, had it been present, would have made Drowne's wooden image instinct with spirit.

The captain of the Cynosure had now finished his instructions.

"And Drowne," said he, impressively, "you must lay aside all other business and set about this forthwith. And as to the price, only do the job in first-rate style, and you shall settle that point yourself."

"Very well, captain," answered the carver, who looked grave and somewhat perplexed, yet had a sort of smile upon his visage; "depend upon it, I'll do my utmost to satisfy you."

From that moment the men of taste about Long Wharf and the Town Dock who were wont to show their love for the arts by frequent visits to Drowne's workshop, and admiration of his wooden images, began to be sensible of a mystery in the carver's conduct. Often he was absent in the daytime. Sometimes, as might be judged by gleams of light from the shop windows, he was at work until a late hour of the evening; although neither knock nor voice, on such occasions, could gain admittance for a visitor, or elicit any word of response. Nothing remarkable, however, was observed in the shop at those late hours when it was thrown open. A fine piece of timber, indeed, which Drowne was known to have reserved for some work of especial dignity, was seen to be gradually assuming shape. What shape it was destined ultimately to take was a problem to his friends and a point on which the carver himself preserved a rigid silence. But day after day, though Drowne was seldom noticed in the act of working upon it, this rude form began to be developed until it became evident to all observers that a female figure was growing into mimic life. At each new visit they beheld a larger pile of wooden chips and a nearer approximation to something beautiful. It seemed as if the hamadryad of the oak had sheltered herself from the unimaginative world within the heart of her native tree, and that it was only necessary to remove the strange shapelessness that had incrusted her, and reveal the grace and loveliness of a divinity. Imperfect as the design, the attitude, the costume, and especially the face of the image still remained, there was already an effect that drew the eye from the wooden cleverness of Drowne's earlier productions and fixed it upon the tantalizing mystery of this new project.

Copley, the celebrated painter, then a young man and a resident of Boston, came one day to visit Drowne; for he had recognized so much of moderate ability in the carver as to induce him, in the dearth of professional sympathy, to cultivate his acquaintance. On entering the shop, the artist glanced at the inflexible image of king, commander, dame, and allegory, that stood around, on the best of which might have been bestowed the questionable praise that it looked as if a living man had here been changed to wood, and that not only the physical, but the intellectual and spiritual part, partook of the stolid transformation. But in not a single instance did it seem as if the wood were imbibing the ethereal essence of humanity. What a wide distinction is here! and how far the slightest portion of the latter merit have outvalued the utmost degree of the former!

"My friend Drowne," said Copley, smiling to himself, but alluding to the mechanical and wooden cleverness that so invariably distinguished the images, "you are really a remarkable person! I have seldom met with a man in your line of business that could do so much; for one other touch might make this figure of General Wolfe, for instance, a breathing and intelligent human creature."

"You would have me think that you are praising me highly, Mr. Copley," answered Drowne, turning his back upon Wolfe's image in apparent disgust. "But there has come a light into my mind. I know what you know as well, that the one touch which you speak of as deficient is the only one that would be truly valuable, and that without it these works of mine are no better than worthless abortions. There is the same difference between them and the works of an inspired artist as between a sign-post daub and one of your best pictures."

"This is strange," cried Copley, looking him in the face, which now, as the painter fancied, had a singular depth of intelligence, though hitherto it had not given him greatly the advantage over his own family of wooden images. "What has come over you? How is it that, possessing the idea which you have now uttered, you should produce only such works as these?"

The carver smiled, but made no reply. Copley turned again to the images, conceiving that the sense of deficiency which Drowne had just expressed, and which is so rare in a merely mechanical character, must surely imply a genius, the tokens of which had heretofore been overlooked. But no; there was not a trace of it. He was about to withdraw when his eyes chanced to fall upon a half-developed figure which lay in a corner of the workshop, surrounded by scattered chips of oak. It arrested him at once.

"What is here? Who has done this?" he broke out, after contemplating it in speechless astonishment for an instant. "Here is the divine, the lifegiving touch. What inspired hand is beckoning this wood to arise and live? Whose work is this?"

"No man's work," replied Drowne. "The figure lies within that block of oak, and it is my business to find it."

"Drowne," said the true artist, grasping the carver fervently by the hand, "you are a man of genius!"

As Copley departed, happening to glance backward from the threshold, he beheld Drowne bending over the half-created shape, and stretching forth his arms as if he would have embraced and drawn it to his heart; while, had such a miracle been possible, his countenance expressed passion enough to communicate warmth and sensibility to the lifeless oak.

"Strange enough!" said the artist to himself. "Who would have looked for a modern Pygmalion in the person of a Yankee mechanic!"

As yet, the image was but vague in its outward presentment; so that, as in the cloud shapes around the western sun, the observer rather felt, or was led to imagine, than really saw what was intended by it. Day by day, however, the work assumed greater precision, and settled its irregular and misty outline into distincter grace and beauty. The general design was now obvious to the common eye. It was a female figure, in what appeared to be a foreign dress; the gown being laced over the bosom, and opening in front so as to disclose a skirt or petticoat, the folds and inequalities of which were admirably represented in the oaken substance. She wore a hat of singular gracefulness, and abundantly laden with flowers, such as never grew in the rude soil of New England, but which, with all their fanciful luxuriance, had a natural truth that it seemed impossible for the most fertile imagination to have attained without copying from real prototypes. There were several little appendages to this dress, such as a fan, a pair of earrings, a chain about the neck, a watch in the bosom, and a ring upon the finger, all of which would have been deemed beneath the dignity of sculpture. They were put on, however, with as much taste as a lovely woman might have shown in her attire, and could therefore have shocked none but a judgment spoiled by artistic rules.

The face was still imperfect; but gradually, by a magic touch, intelligence and sensibility brightened through the features, with all the effect of light gleaming forth from within the solid oak. The face became alive. It was a beautiful, though not precisely regular and somewhat haughty aspect, but with a certain piquancy about the eyes and mouth, which, of all expressions, would have seemed the most impossible to throw over a wooden countenance. And now, so far as carving went, this wonderful production was complete.

"Drowne," said Copley, who had hardly missed a single day in his visits to the carver's workshop, "if this work were in marble it would make you famous at once; nay, I would almost affirm that it would make an era in the art. It is as ideal as an antique statue, and yet as real as any lovely woman whom one meets at a fireside or in the street. But I trust you do not mean to desecrate this exquisite creature with paint, like those staring kings and admirals yonder?"

"Not paint her!" exclaimed Captain Hunnewell, who stood by; "not paint the figure-head of the Cynosure! And what sort of a figure should I cut in a foreign port with such an unpainted oaken stick as this over my prow! She must, and she shall, be painted to the life, from the topmost flower in her hat down to the silver spangles on her slippers."

"Mr. Copley," said Drowne, quietly, "I know nothing of marble statuary, and nothing of the sculptor's rules of art; but of this wooden image, this work of my hands, this creature of my heart,"--and here his voice faltered and choked in a very singular manner,--"of this--of her --I may say that I know something. A well-spring of inward wisdom gushed within me as I wrought upon the oak with my whole strength, and soul, and faith. Let others do what they may with marble, and adopt what rules they choose. If I can produce my desired effect by painted wood, those rules are not for me, and I have a right to disregard them."

"The very spirit of genius," muttered Copley to himself. "How otherwise should this carver feel himself entitled to transcend all rules, and make me ashamed of quoting them?"

He looked earnestly at Drowne, and again saw that expression of human love which, in a spiritual sense, as the artist could not help imagining, was the secret of the life that had been breathed into this block of wood.

The carver, still in the same secrecy that marked all his operations upon this mysterious image, proceeded to paint the habiliments in their proper colors, and the countenance with Nature's red and white. When all was finished he threw open his workshop, and admitted the towns people to behold what he had done. Most persons, at their first entrance, felt impelled to remove their hats, and pay such reverence as was due to the richly-dressed and beautiful young lady who seemed to stand in a corner of the room, with oaken chips and shavings scattered at her feet. Then came a sensation of fear; as if, not being actually human, yet so like humanity, she must therefore be something preternatural. There was, in truth, an indefinable air and expression that might reasonably induce the query, Who and from what sphere this daughter of the oak should be? The strange, rich flowers of Eden on her head; the complexion, so much deeper and more brilliant than those of our native beauties; the foreign, as it seemed, and fantastic garb, yet not too fantastic to be worn decorously in the street; the delicately-wrought embroidery of the skirt; the broad gold chain about her neck; the curious ring upon her finger; the fan, so exquisitely sculptured in open work, and painted to resemble pearl and ebony;--where could Drowne, in his sober walk of life, have beheld the vision here so matchlessly embodied! And then her face! In the dark eyes, and around the voluptuous mouth, there played a look made up of pride, coquetry, and a gleam of mirthfulness, which impressed Copley with the idea that the image was secretly enjoying the perplexing admiration of himself and other beholders.

"And will you," said he to the carver, "permit this masterpiece to become the figure-head of a vessel? Give the honest captain yonder figure of Britannia--it will answer his purpose far better--and send this fairy queen to England, where, for aught I know, it may bring you a thousand pounds."

"I have not wrought it for money," said Drowne.

"What sort of a fellow is this!" thought Copley. "A Yankee, and throw away the chance of making his fortune! He has gone mad; and thence has come this gleam of genius."

There was still further proof of Drowne's lunacy, if credit

were due to the rumor that he had been seen kneeling at the feet of the oaken lady, and gazing with a lover's passionate ardor into the face that his own hands had created. The bigots of the day hinted that it would be no matter of surprise if an evil spirit were allowed to enter this beautiful form, and seduce the carver to destruction.

The fame of the image spread far and wide. The inhabitants visited it so universally, that after a few days of exhibition there was hardly an old man or a child who had not become minutely familiar with its aspect. Even had the story of Drowne's wooden image ended here, its celebrity might have been prolonged for many years by the reminiscences of those who looked upon it in their childhood, and saw nothing else so beautiful in after life. But the town was now astounded by an event, the narrative of which has formed itself into one of the most singular legends that are yet to be met with in the traditionary chimney corners of the New England metropolis, where old men and women sit dreaming of the past, and wag their heads at the dreamers of the present and the future.

One fine morning, just before the departure of the Cynosure on her second voyage to Fayal, the commander of that gallant vessel was seen to issue from his residence in Hanover Street. He was stylishly dressed in a blue broadcloth coat, with gold lace at the seams and button-holes, an embroidered scarlet waistcoat, a triangular hat, with a loop and broad binding of gold, and wore a silver-hilted hanger at his side. But the good captain might have been arrayed in the robes of a prince or the rags of a beggar, without in either case attracting notice, while obscured by such a companion as now leaned on his arm. The people in the street started, rubbed their eyes, and either leaped aside from their path, or stood as if transfixed to wood or marble in astonishment.

"Do you see it?--do you see it?" cried one, with tremulous eagerness. "It is the very same!"

"The same?" answered another, who had arrived in town only the night before. "Who do you mean? I see only a sea-captain in his shoregoing clothes, and a young lady in a foreign habit, with a bunch of beautiful flowers in her hat. On my word, she is as fair and bright a damsel as my eyes have looked on this many a day!"

"Yes; the same!--the very same!" repeated the other. "Drowne's wooden image has come to life!"

Here was a miracle indeed! Yet, illuminated by the sunshine, or darkened by the alternate shade of the houses, and with its garments fluttering lightly in the morning breeze, there passed the image along the street. It was exactly and minutely the shape, the garb, and the face which the towns-people had so recently thronged to see and admire. Not a rich flower upon her head, not a single leaf, but had had its prototype in Drowne's wooden workmanship, although now their fragile grace had become flexible, and was shaken by every footstep that the wearer made. The broad gold chain upon the neck was identical with the one represented on the image, and glistened with the motion imparted by the rise and fall of the bosom which it decorated. A real diamond sparkled on her finger. In her right hand she bore a pearl and ebony fan, which she flourished with a fantastic and bewitching coquetry, that was likewise expressed in all her movements as well as in the style of her beauty and the attire that so well harmonized with it. The face with its brilliant depth of complexion had the same piquancy of mirthful mischief that was fixed upon the countenance of the image, but which was here varied and continually shifting, yet always essentially the same, like the sunny gleam upon a bubbling fountain. On the whole, there was something so airy and yet so real in the figure, and withal so perfectly did it represent Drowne's image, that people knew not whether to suppose the magic wood etherealized into a spirit or warmed and softened into an actual woman.

"One thing is certain," muttered a Puritan of the old stamp, "Drowne has sold himself to the devil; and doubtless this gay Captain Hunnewell is a party to the bargain."

"And I," said a young man who overheard him, "would almost consent to be the third victim, for the liberty of saluting those lovely lips."

"And so would I," said Copley, the painter, "for the privilege of taking her picture."

The image, or the apparition, whichever it might be, still escorted by the bold captain, proceeded from Hanover Street through some of the cross lanes that make this portion of the town so intricate, to Ann Street, thence into Dock Square, and so downward to Drowne's shop, which stood just on the water's edge. The crowd still followed, gathering volume as it rolled along. Never had a modern miracle occurred in such broad daylight, nor in the presence of such a multitude of witnesses. The airy image, as if conscious that she was the object of the murmurs and disturbance that swelled behind her, appeared slightly vexed and flustered, yet still in a manner consistent with the light vivacity and sportive mischief that were written in her countenance. She was observed to flutter her fan with such vehement rapidity that the elaborate delicacy of its workmanship gave way, and it remained broken in her hand.

Arriving at Drowne's door, while the captain threw it open, the marvellous apparition paused an instant on the threshold, assuming the very attitude of the image, and casting over the crowd that glance of sunny coquetry which all remembered on the face of the oaken lady. She and her cavalier then disappeared.

"Ah!" murmured the crowd, drawing a deep breath, as with one vast pair of lungs.

"The world looks darker now that she has vanished," said

some of the young men.

But the aged, whose recollections dated as far back as witch times, shook their heads, and hinted that our forefathers would have thought it a pious deed to burn the daughter of the oak with fire.

"If she be other than a bubble of the elements," exclaimed Copley, "I must look upon her face again."

He accordingly entered the shop; and there, in her usual corner, stood the image, gazing at him, as it might seem, with the very same expression of mirthful mischief that had been the farewell look of the apparition when, but a moment before, she turned her face towards the crowd. The carver stood beside his creation mending the beautiful fan, which by some accident was broken in her hand. But there was no longer any motion in the lifelike image, nor any real woman in the workshop, nor even the witchcraft of a sunny shadow, that might have deluded people's eyes as it flitted along the street. Captain Hunnewell, too, had vanished. His hoarse sea-breezy tones, however, were audible on the other side of a door that opened upon the water.

"Sit down in the stern sheets, my lady," said the gallant captain. "Come, bear a hand, you lubbers, and set us on board in the turning of a minute-glass."

And then was heard the stroke of oars.

"Drowne," said Copley with a smile of intelligence, "you have been a truly fortunate man. What painter or statuary ever had such a subject! No wonder that she inspired a genius into you, and first created the artist who afterwards created her image."

Drowne looked at him with a visage that bore the traces of tears, but from which the light of imagination and sensibility, so recently illuminating it, had departed. He was again the mechanical carver that he had been known to be all his lifetime.

"I hardly understand what you mean, Mr. Copley," said he, putting his hand to his brow. "This image! Can it have been my work? Well, I have wrought it in a kind of dream; and now that I am broad awake I must set about finishing yonder figure of Admiral Vernon."

And forthwith he employed himself on the stolid countenance of one of his wooden progeny, and completed it in his own mechanical style, from which he was never known afterwards to deviate. He followed his business industriously for many years, acquired a competence, and in the latter part of his life attained to a dignified station in the church, being remembered in records and traditions as Deacon Drowne, the carver. One of his productions, an Indian chief, gilded all over, stood during the better part of a century on the cupola of the Province House, bedazzling the eyes of those who looked upward, like an angel of the sun. Another work of the good deacon's hand--a reduced likeness of his friend Captain Hunnewell, holding a telescope and quadrant--may be seen to this day, at the corner of Broad and State streets, serving in the useful capacity of sign to the shop of a nautical instrument maker. We know not how to account for the inferiority of this quaint old figure, as compared with the recorded excellence of the Oaken Lady, unless on the supposition that in every human spirit there is imagination, sensibility, creative power, genius, which, according to circumstances, may either be developed in this world, or shrouded in a mask of dulness until another state of being. To our friend Drowne there came a brief season of excitement, kindled by love. It rendered him a genius for that one occasion, but, quenched in disappointment, left him again the mechanical carver in wood, without the power even of appreciating the work that his own hands had wrought. Yet who can doubt that the very highest state to which a human spirit can attain, in its loftiest aspirations, is its truest

     An Old Woman's Tale and other writings

and most natural state, and that Drowne was more consistent with himself when he wrought the admirable figure of the mysterious lady, than when he perpetrated a whole progeny of blockheads?

There was a rumor in Boston, about this period, that a young Portuguese lady of rank, on some occasion of political or domestic disquietude, had fled from her home in Fayal and put herself under the protection of Captain Hunnewell, on board of whose vessel, and at whose residence, she was sheltered until a change of affairs. This fair stranger must have been the original of Drowne's Wooden Image.

www.ingramcontent.com/pod-product-compliance
Lightning Source LLC
LaVergne TN
LVHW091544170726
843492LV00007B/2086

Justo antes ... ecer

Poemas escogidos

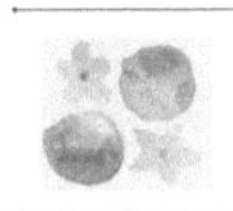

Carlos Almira Picazo

Caminos que a ninguna parte llevan,
entre dos prados;
que, con arte, diríase,
de su destino fueron desviados.

Caminos que no tienen ante sí,
nada más
que el puro espacio,
y la estación.

R.M. Rilke.

EL PEÓN

Entre las cinco y las seis de la mañana,
estoy en Libertad Condicional.
El mismo silencio, la casa y la calle
logra casi hermanar.

No tengo que fingir. Algo más grande que yo
me roza. No necesito nada más.
Dentro de la noche aún, la casa y la calle,
baña la misma claridad.

En el tablero del poderoso -la partida está dispuesta-
soy el peón que falta en la caja.

EMPRENDEDORES

¿Qué puedes hacer?
Un buen currículo.
Escribir un soneto.
-Tal vez los de arriba se conmuevan-.
Aprender inglés.
No para leer Hamlet,
sino para hacer camas
y fregar vómitos en los hoteles.
Sonreír, apretando bien los puños.
Sacarte el carné de conducir.
Ser siempre joven y emprendedor.
Ir a la universidad. Buscar pareja.
Hacer lo que tus viejos no pudieron hacer,
y olvidarles.
Volver al pueblo donde creciste,
por el águila muerta junto a una acequia,
con el anillo del Zoo de Estocolmo en una pata.
"Desde hace algún tiempo, aunque no sé por qué,
he perdido mi antigua alegría
y he dejado mis viejas ocupaciones.
Y la tierra, con toda su maravillosa maquinaria,
no me parece sino un estéril promontorio".
Acaso el día de mañana traiga la Justicia.

A MI CARTERA DE PROFESOR

Cuando me libere, te sacaré todos los libros,
los papeles y las carpetas; el lastre de estos años.
Los arañazos de tu piel, y tus correas pasadas
podrán descansar; como mi voz y mis ojos.
¡Lo prometo! Recobrarás tu vida, callada y verdadera;
como yo, el movimiento precioso de las calles.
Quien quiera aprender en adelante, que busque en sí mismo.
¡Horarios, clases, cuadernos del profesor, todo a la basura!
Aligerada del fardo, podrás levantar al fin el vuelo.
Y yo, oír en la resonancia del silencio así ganado, mi alma.
Y pasar de la muerte en vida a la inmensidad.

LECHUGA

Se sentaba en un banco de la primera fila,
aunque no la recuerdas nunca la has olvidado:
el nido de su pelo aún cae arremolinado
 como un escalofrío dentro de tu pupila.

Nocturno fluorescente: cae una lluvia tranquila;
aunque ya no la olvidas nunca la has recordado;
se sentaba y la puerta se entreabría a su lado;
un fragor de jardín temblaba en su pupila.

Nunca hablasteis: el hola y el adios de rigor;
sus hombros, sus caderas, su melena esparcida,
es todo lo que queda de aquel nocturno triste.

Ni un nombre, ni una cara, ni una voz, ni un olor;
aunque no la recuerdas sabes que la perdiste
como un día, como un día cualquiera de tu vida.

FUTBOLINES

Es hora de clase: en la sala desierta
moscas en los vasos, un almanaque, frío;
libros arrumbados, voces junto a la puerta;
la Derby con su trueno, la calle como un río.

No hay futuro: más allá la mañana entreabierta,
vergeles en los ojos, zarpa para el vacío;
nunca más en las voces; en la escollera muerta
de las manos, un algo azul como un envío.

Futbolines, edénicos prados del billar;
cada segundo un oh! negro como un zarpazo;
el Play Boy, polizón triste de la cartera.

Non future: los ojos a punto de zarpar;
y "dime que me quieres", mientras dura el abrazo;
y la lluvia, la noche, al acecho allá afuera.

UN LIBRO USADO

Que des jours passés une fois de plus sous le silence!
Así lo encontré, subrayado en un libro de Kafka,
encontrado por azar en una librería de viejo, hace unos días.
Más tarde, ya en casa, dentro de las páginas,
vi el cartón que servía de pasa-páginas, una entrada de cine du
Centre Pompidou,
cortada, doce años atrás, por unas manos desconocidas.
¡Ah, estas líneas misteriosamente subrayadas,
por esas manos! ¿De quién? ¿Para qué?
Que des jours passés une fois de plus sous le silence!, como un
mensaje de amor.
Cuánto me hablan, cuánto me dicen de mi vida de ahora.
Esas manos perdidas entre las palabras en francés, de un libro
desgastado, por el roce del amor.
Cómo llegan hasta mí y me hablan a través de la hondura del
Tiempo insondable.
Et toutes ces nuits, sais tu, dans toutes ces maisons!

Me gustaría encontrar al dueño de esas manos.
Y decirle: gracias, simplemente, gracias.
En la felicidad de los jardines.
En la calma de mi habitación en penumbra, esta noche.
Si la vida pudiera enseñarnos algo, y fuéramos capaces de
retenerlo un segundo,
en los objetos que tocaron, que acariciaron insospechados
mensajeros.
Gracias por recordarme la felicidad de estar perdido en el Tiempo.
Por todas esas noches, ¿lo sabías?, que entran en las casas.
Por todos esos días pasados una y otra vez, bajo el silencio.
Así intenté traducir las palabras, como la primavera traduce los
árboles.
Como hacen a veces las nubes, con el alfabeto invisible del cielo.
Y continúo la cadena del aire feliz, que nadie ha empezado.
Porque unas manos desconocidas subrayaron estas palabras en un
libro usado,
hallado por azar, en una librería de viejo, en Granada,
con la foto de Kafka en la portada, en blanco y negro, ensimismado
en una nostalgia incurable,
como si también él pudiera oír el bullicio de las calles junto al
Sena, y verme en mi habitación doce años después>.
Me desharé un día en un abrazo, Et tous ces jours passés sous le
silence!, con un desconocido.

EN EL PASEO DE LA BOMBA

Cuando nuestros años sean sólo memoria, una anécdota,
pervivirá la escena a que asistimos tantas veces:
padre e hija, subiendo y bajando del brazo, por el Paseo de la
Bomba.

Él lee. La mano libre, juega de vez en cuando como un animalillo,
con el pelo de ella;
acompasándose al andar, corto y errático, de la joven;
dueño ya de algo que nada puede darle ni quitarle en este mundo.
El calor, la respiración heridos del ser vivo.

Cuando nuestros años sean sólo memoria, apenas una anécdota.
Y nuestra vejez, vuelta de repente, por un instante, juventud por
el afecto,
reviva la escena, a que asistimos tantas veces, en el Paseo de la
Bomba.

EL AUTOBÚS

Voy solo, en el autobús medio vacío.
Todos están en el trabajo, o de compras.
Las calles huyen de la ventanilla con extrañeza.
Viajo casi solo. Ya voy de vuelta a casa.

Quién pudiera realizar lo inevitable en su vida,
vivir, en vez de estar esperando continuamente un milagro:
pues todo momento es engañoso;
cada encuentro; cada mirada.

En esto voy pensando en el autobús, a deshoras.
Con toda la resonancia de la mañana. Casi solo.
Y con una nostalgia incurable,
como un Rey tendido en un sarcófago antiguo.

LA ENRAMADA

Tu silencio me cerca. Pero tú y yo sabemos
que los años del mundo no pueden separarnos.
Es demasiado tarde. ¿Tendremos que encontrarnos
en la casualidad, que nunca entenderemos?

Yo te haré una señal, y no nos miraremos.
Y sonará el teléfono de noche, al acostarnos.
Estaremos tan lejos que querremos tocarnos.
Y, sin decirnos nada, todo nos lo diremos.

Tu silencio me cerca, como una onda oscura
que crece, derrumbándose. Pero tú y yo sabemos
que los años del mundo no pueden hacer nada.

No pueden hacer nada, ni con toda su hondura.
En la misma enramada, abrazados iremos.
Abrazados iremos, en la misma enramada.

LO AUTÉNTICO

Cuando las tardes empiecen a ser más largas,
quizá te haga una visita. Un día de estos.
Entonces gritaré: ¡ahora o nunca!"

Nada ha cambiado. Aunque te empeñas en vivir
como el artesano en su obra de arte. Lo auténtico
pasa. Sólo la muerte se repite.

MONTEFRÍO

La carretera de Córdoba
se esconde por Montefrío.
Por allí pasé, seis años
que hoy no me parecen míos.

La carretera de Córdoba
se pierde, hacia Puerto Lope.
Todavía. ¿Viviremos
cuando ya nadie nos nombre?

La carretera de Córdoba:
entre encinas, entre olivos.
Por allí pasé seis años,
que hoy no me parecen míos.

Todavía viviremos,
cuando ya nadie nos nombre:
por las curvas; en la brisa
que se pierde por los montes.

HISTORIA UNIVERSAL

Hoy me conmovieron tus macetas, tan valientes en la ventana,
al aparecer a la luz del tubo fluorescente de la cocina;
mientras hervía el café; tan pequeñas y tan solas:
el hinojo, el rosal, la margarita; en el filo de la noche.

Cada hoja; cada flor; cada ramita, tanteaban afuera:
el perro; el cuco; el coche, intermitentes en el silencio.

Cuando hayamos abandonado nuestro puesto, pensé:
ellas seguirán ahí; cada hoja; cada flor; cada ramita;
como un dique, intrépidas, conteniendo el mundo en resaca.
Tanteando con ingenua incredulidad lo insondable.

EL ÚLTIMO HOMBRE

El último hombre se tumbará en el suelo.
Y, en posición horizontal, como una canoa,
se dejará surcar por las aguas invisibles.

Sus ojos cerrados, se llenarán de estrellas.
Sonreirá de puro triste. La respiración tranquila,
se acompasará con el movimiento leve de las piernas.

Las manos inservibles, yacerán como objetos preciosos,
expuestos, como las alas de un pájaro que duerme.

EL TIEMPO

Todos estamos en el Tiempo,
algunos años de nuestra vida.

Un sol apagado, corto.
Un muro pequeño.
Un campo que despierta la helada.

EL RÍO

Ayer arrancaron la maleza del río.
Y esta mañana, cuando íbamos al colegio,
había un camión listo para llevársela.
La orilla quedó desnuda de su sombra inquieta.

Los países se deshacen en pocos minutos.
Abrirán el portalón, y nos separaremos
hasta el medio día. Entonces el camión
ya no estará. Pero bajo tierra,
se tejerá ya el vestido nuevo del aire.

CUCARACHAS

No dejes de tocar la guitarra.
Toda la casa tiene miedo.
Y sobre todo, tu habitación.

¿Qué harás con las manos después?
La calle contiene un aliento helado,
donde ya se forma un ejército de cucarachas,
que sube por las hendiduras del silencio.

ENTONCES

Cuando llegues cansado del trabajo, dentro de muchos años,
extraño a lo que eres, malbaratado por el día;
escucha y recuerda cómo sonaba la guitarra eléctrica de Charley;
dentro de muchos años, tal y como serás entonces, en la misma
casa pero con otra vida;
como algo que estaba escrito en ti, con todo lo que eras desde
siempre;
como las estrellas en el pozo callado y verde que flota dentro del
hombre;
en los barcos que resbalan por los ojos tranquilos y cerrados de la
noche;
cuando llegues cansado y recuerdes cómo era aquella música
entonces.

HIC ET NUNC

Es ahora o nunca.
Haz lo que tengas que hacer.
Para que mañana no tengas que arrepentirte de nada,
en el silencio de tu cuarto,
al fondo de una calle, solo.

Este es el momento.
No habrá otro, cuando en tu cuarto,
solo, te encuentres en el espejo,
mañana,-sólo la seda podrá arañar tu nuca-,
con la antigua lejanía.

RILKE

En uno de los puestos que ponían
en la Carrera de la Virgen, cuando
yo empezaba a escribir, encontré un día
un libro, con los versos de Rilke.

Si vivir es algo que no elegimos,
y que perdemos enseguida, presos del hábito,
como se escapa el humo o el vaho; la vida
nos salva a veces. Y en algún momento,
yo sentí tu mano cálida, en la nuca,
al pasar las páginas,
con todo lo dulce que puede contener la sombra.

REQUIEM

No sé cómo voy a vivir los años que me faltan,
con tu habitación y tus cuadernos infantiles
vacíos, y sin poder besarte la frente.

Tendrán que pasar despacio, muy despacio
por nuestra calle, como mi ataúd.

LA FAROLA

La farola, ¡qué lejos
del trasiego de las calles!
Apenas un rasguño dorado,
en el frío del parque.

Recogida, íntima,
perdida,
¿en qué visiones solitarias?

ARQUEOLOGÍA

Niños. Nacían de nuestra mirada
las calles. Y en el juego eran semilla.
Las cuentas en la mesa. Oscurecíanse
los vidrios. Y entraban en el vasto sueño.

Fuera, sólo el trabajo de vivir. El arte.
Los días. La renuncia. El fuego.
Por los caminos olvidados.

MAMÁ

Estás mayor. No coges el teléfono.
Y el televisor retumba en toda la casa.
Nadie viene a verte. Pero las tardes no son tristes.
Es algo que pasa. Uno envejece.

Todos los pueblos donde fuiste maestra,
han salido a la luz, a la superficie, en los pantanos,
por la sequía. Incluso el aire para los pájaros.
Aunque sólo las nubes son reales.

Yo he seguido los pasos de papá
muchos años. Pero ya me cansan los libros.
Siento miles de hormigas subir por mi cuerpo cada noche.
Y busco la rima que nos justifique,
como la brizna de hierba en los escalones del Partenom.

1984

En el ochenta y cuatro yo acababa
de iniciarme en la vida de estudiante.
Nos llevará la vida por delante,
como esta lluvia, un día. Así pensaba.

E intuía a un ser que respiraba
en la cáscara dulce del instante.
Y rimaba lo cursi y lo pedante
que, a veces, una chispa me arrancaba.

Iba entre los demás sin darme cuenta.
Me embebía en la calle la onda rubia
del dios, que hace que el mundo se nos abra.

Y la vida era dulce, triste, lenta.
Un verso que buscaba una palabra
en la melena suelta de la lluvia.

DIOS

He vivido con los ojos cerrados,
bordeando un precipicio.
Entre el esplendor de la verdad,
y el olvido que hace posible cada día.

A Dios nadie lo ha visto,
y nadie lo verá.
Sólo los niños pueden tocarlo.

Como un relámpago furtivo, se desliza
entre los dedos de un moribundo,
por toda la Eternidad.

EL COMPAÑERO POETA

En el último curso nocturno del Instituto
escribía poemas. Siempre solo. De negro.
Flaco. En los pasillos. Al evocarlo ahora,
te sale al encuentro el joven que fuiste,
desvanecido. Y recuerdas la cicatriz de su cara.

Cuántas veces, al conjurarlo después, te topaste
con tu vida de entonces. Aunque ahora sabes
que no es él, sino tu emoción, lo único que pervive.
Como el verde de las islas en el mar antiguo.

ESCENA

Ahora estarás durmiendo, mientras papá apura
el café, el cigarrillo. Los restos de la mesa
tendrán esa nostalgia de la costumbre; esa
tristeza, que los años ponen en lo que dura.

La casa, con la tarde, se pondrá más oscura.
Y habrá por Santa Cruz un barco que regresa.
Cuando al anochecer, nuestra infancia en la mesa,
buscará también puerto, y caricia segura.

Habrá un ruido ligero por la calle dormida.
Y hacia el anochecer, las sombras por la casa,
esconderán los pájaros, tenues de remembranza.

Luego despertarás, y será nuestra vida:
como el sol que germina; como el tiempo que pasa.
Vuelta para el olvido y la desesperanza.

NOSTALGIA

Ellos serán pequeños otra vez.
Y buscarás piojos en sus cabezas,
hechas para reclinarse. El sueño.

El frío espantará a las últimas moscas,
escondido en los ojos, como un presagio.

PLAN DE VIDA

Paséate solo por las noches,
aunque estés a muchos kilómetros del mar.
Canta sólo para ti. No molestes.
Puede que al final entiendas algo.

Cuando los años te saquen del tiempo,
que te encuentren solo, irreconocible;
desnudo; limpio; como un campo arado.

PLAN DE VIDA 2

Cuando apriete el calor, bajaremos al río,
donde se dan cita aguas inmemoriales;
y se bañan golfillos y parejas con perro.
Y la tarde de agosto se llevará a Granada.

Interminablemente, se anunciará el otoño
en las cafeterías y las nubes del centro.
Huérfanos de los hijos, lejos: donde las aguas;
los árboles; el aire, a aprender el olvido.

KAVAFIS

Horas de trabajo, amor y estudio,
enseñan sus páginas. Toda una vida
de dedicación al arte de la Poesía.

Cada verso trasluce una emoción,
como el primer sol de la mañana en una calle.

LA CABINA

Quiero llamarte desde la cabina
que tenía mi calle, y me respondas.
Que tu voz viaje por las negras ondas,
donde todo comienza y se termina.

Antes de separarnos en la esquina,
te besaré con lengua. No te escondas.
El tráfico, por calles y rotondas,
resonará como una concertina.

Con la verdad del mundo, te conjuro,
ahora o nunca, desde un ayer futuro:
ven como eras, como siempre fuiste.

Yo estaré en la cabina que tú sabes,
esperando tu voz. Las rachas suaves
de la lluvia. La noche. Solo y triste.

LA ESPERA

No tener piel.
Sentirlo todo.
En la larga despedida,
cimentar la espera.

La espera de algo,
que canta en las hojas.

ILION

¿Qué les diré a mis alumnos?
Un día fui como vosotros.
Nada volverá nunca. Nada.

Hice lo que pude.
Me arrastró el tiempo,
como un carro de bronce.

LA OCASIÓN

Cuando se te presente la ocasión
sal, como si fueras el dueño de tu vida.
En realidad lo eres, en lo más hondo de tu ser,
allí donde no llega la necesidad.

Sal. Y, libre entre los que se venden
por no estar solos, busca la placita que tú sabes,
con su terraza, desierta en plena jornada laboral,
y, aunque sólo sea por una hora, permanece fuera de la Historia.

RELLANOS

Me gusta cuando hacemos el amor
los lunes por la tarde. Me gusta
cuando llueve y no llevo paraguas,
y cuando me escuchas como a un niño.

Me gusta cuando Julia canta sola en su cuarto,
creyendo que no la oye nadie. Y cuando
no te das cuenta de que no llevo calcetines.

Me gusta bajar andando los rellanos de las escaleras.
El olor, la luz ausente que hay en los pisos.
Y las escopetas de perdigones de las ferias de mi memoria.

HORIZONTE

Como un puente que cruza los dos ojos.
Como un río verde, estoy sentado
en el quicio de una puerta cerrada.

He esperado toda mi vida,
el momento feliz del horizonte
en que, joven otra vez, tendré una sombra.

Me siento como tú ahora. Solo.
Y te pierdo, y te recobro entre sedas.
En el quicio feliz del horizonte.

MILAGRO DE LA POESÍA

Al fin soy yo. Me reconozco.
Milagro de la poesía.
En todo lo que no lleva mi nombre.

LA NADA

Aprovecha las horas de la tarde
para escribir, mientras aún puedas
insuflar un poco de vida en tus palabras,
y transmitir, así, una emoción.

Aunque nadie te lo exija, aprovecha para escribir
cada momento de la tarde.
La casa y tú, al fin solos.
Tu soledad intacta, como en la adolescencia.

Cuando ya no exista el mundo,
que al menos el silencio, el vacío,
puedan estremecerse en los vastos espacios,
y ya no sea posible la Nada.

TU MÚSICA

Vengo escuchando tu música,
por lugares donde he sido feliz
hace cuarenta, cuarenta y cinco años.
En una segunda juventud, vengo contigo,
pasajero en una onda feliz de música
donde estás solo, invisible como el amor;
por los siglos de los siglos, y fuera del tiempo;
por lugares donde he sido feliz.

De pronto estoy en la Avenida América,
delante del bloque amarillo donde viví de joven;
cambiado por dentro y por fuera, junto al nuevo
subterráneo, que emerge de pronto en la mitad de la avenida;
empujado por el tráfico que corre hacia el centro;
sintiéndome como hace mucho que no me sentía: real,
libre y feliz, con tu música sonando en el salpicadero.
Feliz, porque aquí también fui desgraciado y casi adolescente;
como todos los hombres heridos por el amor;
contigo invisible a mi lado, fuera del tiempo.

Todo aparece de golpe en la ventanilla,
y resbala en imágenes, como el agua de la Alhambra,

feliz por el oscuro de los cipreses de algún domingo

de mi adolescencia; feliz como yo oyendo tu música;
y cantándolo con estas palabras, como podría cantarlo con otras;
para abrirme camino hacia adentro y hacia afuera de mí mismo;
para abrirme un boquete por donde pueda respirar el mundo.
Como el agua de la Alhambra, feliz por el color oscuro de los
cipreses,
las tardes de algunos domingos de mi adolescencia;
sintiéndome como hacía mucho tiempo que no me sentía: real y
libre.

Y todo queda atrás,
para formar al fin un océano cada vez más oscuro.
Fui herido por la vida, y eso me dio fuerzas,
hasta que comprendí que todo está hecho del mismo olvido
que separa lo real de lo puramente imaginario:
en la ropa, en los cajones; con los libros en sus estantes;
entre los muebles, en la madrugada.
Una noche que dormía todo yo me desperté cantándote,
en la casa donde viví cuando era joven;
en las calles que recorrí maquinalmente, cuando era joven.
Pasajero en una onda feliz de música y olvido.

INVISIBLE

Muchas veces, invisible
en lo que eras, pasabas
como un poco de paisaje;
pues la mayoría ignora
lo que otros no han nombrado.

Y, en tu gran soledad,
te sentías vivo, como
cerca de la muerte: entre
sus voces, como silencio;
y entre sus cuerpos, como aire.

LA AMERICANA

Dónde estará la americana,
color humo de tabaco,
que, en mi adolescencia lejana,
heredé yo de mi tío Paco.

Cuando las finas madrugadas,
con sus imágenes borrosas
me insinuaban, encantadas,
el secreto de todas las cosas.

Dónde estará la americana,
color de humo de tabaco,
que, en mi adolescencia lejana,
heredé yo de mi tío Paco.

EL SUEÑO

Cuando duermes, el mundo cae en el frío.
Y hay galaxias encerradas en cada haz
de luz, desmoronándose por los rincones.
El sueño es una cárcel, como las estaciones,
en el lecho de un río.

Hace frío en el mundo que me dejas. Sombrío
hierro. Y un eco recorre nuestras habitaciones.
Cuando duermes, me rompo contra los malecones,
amor herido por el frío.

Intento sacudirte.
El sueño es como un eco que recorre la casa.
Y en las rendijas de tus ojos, vasto como el océano,
hay un jardín hundido.

No encuentro la canción. Has tenido que irte.
Me has dejado la noche, como un viento que pasa.
Herido por el sueño, amor, por el frío herido.

LAS BALLENAS

Me gusta cuando hablamos y me miras,
y entre los muebles pasan las ballenas.
En el fragor marino, muero joven.

MATRONAS

Cargadas de bolsas y de achaques, pero inquebrantables;
en el autobús o en el supermercado;
abuelas del barrio del Zaidín o de los Vergeles,
recias, como matronas de los tiempos antiguos.

No una estirpe de héroes, sino de trabajadores
y estudiantes distéis; de niño, yo corrí entre vosotras
antes de convertirme en un joven solitario,
por las mismas calles que ahora, cobran vida al veros.

Cuando quieran quitarnos lo que es nuestro, tendrán
que pasar por encima de vosotras, en vuestras Termóphilas;
sencillas, antes de que se abra el precipicio un día.

Y se oirá en las escaleras el canario, y la radio apagada;
y flotará el olor de las cocinas entre las macetas;
y las calles se llenarán de niños de cincuenta años.

PALABRAS PARA CARLOS

No bajes de las ramas, de los árboles altos
donde se ondula el día.
El tiempo, con la muerte, te acecha entre los troncos.
No bajes de las ramas.

Todos tus compañeros, tus amigos, se han ido.
Si a veces te recuerdan, es con lástima irónica.
No reniegues nunca de las ramas; defiende
hasta el último aliento, su susurro insondable.

Allá abajo el mundo pertenece a los otros.
Que la muerte te encuentre feliz, entre las hojas.
Como mueren las nubes cuando llora la lluvia.
Que tus días se pierdan como el agua que corre.

Hilvanando el espacio, hasta la última estrella;
ancho como el olvido donde se abre la rosa.

SOCIEDAD

Un plato con roscos de azúcar,
colmado, calientes todavía;
regalo de nuestros vecinos; ¿a cambio?:
de vivir puerta con puerta, aquí enfrente;
de ser amables en el ascensor, en las escaleras;
de hablar del tiempo; de preguntar por los nietos;
con toda naturalidad, como cuando respiras;
un plato colmado de roscos de azúcar.

MODERNISMO

A Charlie

Ser joven otra vez, y mirar por encima
del hombro, los arriates de un verdor insolente.
No votar nunca. Hablar del gobierno y la gente.
Vagar por una calle, mascullando una rima.

Devorar cada noche un libro diferente.
Fumar como un obrero, y beber gin con lima.
Despreciar el amor, hondo como una sima,
con el diablo en el cuerpo, y un ángel en la frente.

Leer todos los libros en la gran soledad
de nuestra habitación, con la ventana abierta,
incluso en invierno, a la misma placita.

Consumir cada instante como la eternidad,
inconscientes del mundo que llama a nuestra puerta.
Y una antigua alegría, y una pena infinita.

LA PERRA

Cada uno va solo, con sus preocupaciones,
como si los demás pudiesen comprenderlo.
Rueda desde que es niño. Se abre paso a empujones.
Finge lo que no es, para así poder serlo.

En secreto, construye jardines y prisiones.
Y hay como un agujero que quiere contenerlo.
Rueda por una calle, perdido en sus razones.
Como si los demás pudiesen entenderlo.

Un día se da cuenta de que todo ha pasado.
La que fuera su musa, la noche, lo encierra.
En miedo, el amor, en su muro encantada.

Donde antes respiraba, ya sólo queda tierra.
Por fin es él. Un día negro como una perra.
Como una perra enferma que se tumba a su lado.

LOS OCHENTA

Son los ochenta. Tengo quince o dieciséis años.
Es una tarde triste de un viernes que se va.
La calle Pedro Antonio. Hacia los aledaños,
alcohólicos que entran y salen de los pubs.

Voy solo, atormentado como se va a esos años.
Con un ansia de lobo que husmea, -¿qué husmeará?-.
Hay placitas recónditas donde desgranan caños,
y flota como un aire de algo que ya no está.

Una obsesión febril de cuerpos femeninos,
voy solo, atiborrado de libros, ¡es la edad!
Con una murria antigua. Hay caños cristalinos.

Siento el paso del tiempo como una oscuridad
que me acecha. Y el mañana, con sus pasos felinos.
Una tarde de un viernes desde la eternidad.

EL CIRCO

Los bárbaros han acampado en los límites
de nuestra infancia. Pronto se hará de noche.
Hay carros y animales en los descampados.
Tiembla el cielo sobre las tiendas de lona.

Un olor a lluvia, como el perfume de un recuerdo,
flota entre las luces borrosas. Furgones de feria.
Perros escuálidos y temibles de la Edad de Hierro.
Como si ya hubiésemos vivido para siempre.

EL CHATARRERO

Soy el hombre de la chatarra.
Me viste muchas veces, de niño,
de paso hacia los descampados
donde acababa tu calle.

Tiraba de mi bicicleta, de un carrito,
con una mezcla de fatiga y hastío;
y un perro, siempre callado, me seguía;
y el aire de no ser de ningún sitio.

Existía porque me mirabas.
Aún llevo conmigo el niño que eras.
Fantasías y miedos, todo ha cambiado,
pero yo sigo siendo el mismo hombre.

El hombre que acarreaba la chatarra;
que pasaba por tu calle cuando eras niño;
con un perro callado, como de otro mundo;
y el aire de no ser de ninguna parte.

DOÑA PETRA

La abuela Petra -Piedra-,
la madre de mi madre,
murió; cerró la casa;
dejó a sus dos maridos,
y sus óleos colgados;
dejó las gachas dulces;
y sus novelitas de Ágata Cristhie;
y a sus perros de compañía;
cogió el metro en Bravo Murillo,
con su cartilla de ahorros
bien guardada en el bolso,
junto a la lotería;
y se fue tan contenta,
como si volviera a su pueblo.

SEÑALES

Hay señales inequívocas de la muerte:
la desorientación temporal;
la dificultad para dormir;
las arrugas inexplicables en la ropa;
la desaparición del sabor de los platos;
la inutilidad repentina de muebles y libros;
la cercanía de plantas y perros;
los restos de comida;
las cartas del banco;
las caras de quienes nos quieren;
el frío, el vaho entre las palabras.

LI BO

Tengo cincuenta y cuatro años.
Centenares de páginas escritas.
No tengo editor.
No tengo lectores.

Así están las cosas.
Será mejor aceptarlo.
¿Por qué no me tomas como aprendiz,
y retocamos esa montaña?

JULIA

Echo de menos los cuentos
y tu cara, y la atención
con que me miras.

Voy a regar las macetas.
El mar se lo llevará todo.

DEJA QUE ME ACURRUQUE

Deja que me acurruque
contra tu cuerpo. Duerme
tranquila. La noche
trae en el pico la madrugada.

Estamos solos. Deja
que me acurruque contra ti.
Que ate la cinta de tu frente,
y ciña tu cuerpo en la niebla.

COLLIURE

Cuando sea mayor y me quiera perder,
llévame de la mano como a un hombre mayor
que ha visto y ha leído lo que había que leer,
y quiere ser el joven que te hacía el amor.

Cuando no hay un mañana ya no importa el ayer.
La verdad evasiva, la emoción sin pudor.
Se abren las horas nuevas casi al anochecer.
El sol, ya frío, revela su caricia mejor.

Dame la mano tibia, cuando el reloj parado,
como una resonancia, con la antigua ceguera,
aulle por el amor perdido y encontrado.

Cuando es tarde, vivir se vuelve una quimera.
El sol calienta apenas sobre un mundo apagado,
este sol de la infancia, y esta muerte extranjera.

PLAN DE VIDA

Escribir poemas.
Pintar cuadros (o paredes).
Fue el plan de vida
que me hice de joven.

¿Lo cumplí? Contra todo
pronóstico, la vida
no se deja cantar,
ni poner en color.

Mi juventud se volvió
pensativo paso, mirada;
invernal silencio.

VERLAINE

En una casa antigua, por el centro,
fumar cuando las tardes estén quietas;
ir a por todas, joven, al encuentro
de caras y miradas indiscretas.

Mirar las calles siempre desde dentro;
en un balcón de hierro con macetas;
en un hotel ambiguo, por el centro,
fumar, cuando las tardes estén quietas.

CADA DÍA

Cada día rompe contra lo que somos,
con lo único que podría liberarnos,
como las olas de un mar verde y vivo.

UNA TARDE

Es una tarde de invierno
antigua como un cristal,
para perder el amor,
para volverlo a encontrar.

CUERPO

¿Qué quieres ahora, viejo? ¿No tuviste bastante
cuando fuerte, invisible, te perdías en la vida?
¿Arrastrarte unos años, apurar el instante,
con tal de no caer en la llama encendida?

Todo tiene su tiempo. Nada vuelve. ¡Adelante!
¿Qué aventura, qué amor, busca tu alma afligida?
¿Qué quieres ahora, viejo? ¿No tuviste bastante
cuando fuerte, sensible, te perdías en la vida?

EDAD DE ORO

Estoy solo, escuchando la lluvia.
Podría estar así los próximos mil años,
pero escribo estos versos,
mientras se forma un atasco fenomenal en la autovía.

La lluvia y la soledad se acabarán pronto,
y vendrá un día azul en que el hombre, curado,
escribirá sus versos como el día talla sus nubes.
Y la brisa de la Edad de Oro le dará en la cara.

EL CÍRCULO

Noche. Dolor. Yo estoy encerrado
en un círculo que no puede romperse.
Luego la mañana saldrá del aire,
en la oscura tranquilidad de la calle. Sólo
yo seguiré encerrado, en un círculo que no puede romperse.

FERNANDO PESSOA

Quiero que nos encontremos.
Que bajemos al Tajo por una calle
que ya no existe. Conformes
con la vejez de las fachadas. Callados
para escuchar mejor la voz. Como
el pájaro recóndito, en el claustro.
Como la lluvia en el tejadillo.
Ser niño otra vez. Mirar los barcos.
Conformes con el pozo del tiempo.
Invisibles como la muchedumbre.
La vida es muy corta.
Apenas un día
que la noche recorta
con su calma fría.
Y además, no importa.

BARRABÁS

Yo no me levanté contra Roma. ¿Qué era Roma?
Un nombre en los libros. Un sueño. Un día vi
en un camino junto al desierto, un lirio.
El primero de la estación que, con trabajo,
se había abierto paso entre las piedras. La misma agua
que corre dulce y fresca, libre; en las vasijas
de los hombres sabe ya amarga. Comprendí
que mis semejantes habían usurpado la tierra,
con sus ciudades y sus mercados. Y tomé las armas.
No por la reflexión, ni la justicia, ni la profecía.
Contra la tristeza del mundo. Sino por ese lirio
morado, ingenuo, solo, en una esquina del día.

JERUSALEM

Un día, presintiendo el final, la muerte,
tomé el camino del sur. Me despedí
de mis amigos; de las gentes sencillas;
de mis huertos; mis pozos. Las mañana se sucedieron
con las noches. Y alcancé el desierto
y el mar del sur. Y me hablaron.

Vi la golondrina de Egipto entre las torres,
como un signo de vida, junto al oasis.
Pude haberme perdido en las montañas;
la nieve; con las grandes caravanas de la India.
Pero preferí entrar en la ciudad. Entre la gente.
Metido en mis pensamientos, en mi silencio.

Una nube de polvo me engulló, extraño,
traspasada la muralla; por las calles angostas.
El agua feliz de los arroyos, fresca y dulce, libre,
sabía amarga en las vasijas de los hombres.
Como un arroyo que salta entre las casas, inconsciente
de su destino, entré sin pensar. Había un perfume rezagado.

Besaba el crepúsculo el desierto. Dios,
mi oasis, se abría en la rosa de la distancia
cuando me prendieron. Mi cuerpo libre por el dolor;
sintió otra vez los huertos, los patios, la soledad.
Como la higuera humilde encerrada en la caja de la noche.
Con una pena más antigua que el mundo.
Con la alegría que ha de despertarlo todo.

POÉTICA

Son mis primeros años de poeta
y escribo, escribo trabajosamente.
Granada es una calle con un puente.
Un tumulto, una paz casi completa.

Hundo mis manos en la fuente quieta
de Machado y Rubén adolescente.
Y bebo como un pájaro de Oriente
el girigay del olmo, su silueta.

De la paleta escojo, fiel, la rima,
cada palabra. El verso libre asoma
encantado de fuentes y de trinos.

Como los ojos dulces de una prima.
Como el olor del campo en una loma.
Como las hojas sobre los caminos.

EL RELLANO

¿Qué nos encontraremos cuando abramos la puerta?
Un silencio de madrugada. Algo completamente nuevo.
La apariencia de otros días. Un poco de mañana
flotando como reseda. Voces por contornos en fuga.

POETA ANTIGUO

Hace calor y no puedo dormir.
Todo está en silencio, deshabitado.
Busco tus poemas, tan antiguos y tan nuevos.
Y los leo en voz baja, para no despertar al día.

Entre los espacios en blanco van las palabras,
su música, hasta el mar, como el primer día.
La vida es una madurez del corazón.

AUTORRETRATO

Carlos Almira Picazo.
Hijo de una maestra y un poeta.
Hecho de silencio. Solo.
Solo para siempre.

Parado en una calle del centro.
A punto de abrazarse las piernas.
Una tarde de julio. Solo.
Como los ojos de los niños.

EL FRÍO

Cómo traeré el sol,
los edificios, las calles,
donde viví a mi manera
de fantasías, de hechos,
y reharé el mundo
donde nos componíamos.

Son los años setenta,
y el picú llena el piso
con poemas de Cohen.
Como una Anunciación
se oscurecen las manos,
las lámparas, el frío, suaves.

BARRABÁS 2

Al hombre yo lo vi por encima del sol,
del ruido, el polvo que llenaban la plaza;
por la pura inocencia, en la sombra del día;
¿me miró?, al resonar mi nombre por el aire.

Fue sólo un instante, pero fue suficiente.
Reducido a estampa, a fábula de niños,
me levanté y me fui por los siglos desiertos;
por el ruido y el polvo que llenaba la plaza.

EL MUEBLE

El mueble le gustó desde el principio:
estrecho, desvalido, con sus cuatro estantes,
en excelente estado; para exponer
las fotografías de la familia o la loza;
muñecas y figuras antiguas, y cosas así;
porcelana, seda, plata, cristal, encerrados
en el aire cansado de la vitrina.

Una extraña vida e inteligencia flota
en el mismo rincón, quieto desde hace años,
en la vaguada de las mañanas, en el silencio de las noches,
como una presencia acogedora.

SITIO

Tengo el sabor intacto de aquel día,
cuando cumplí los quince años
y me emborraché con vino de Costa,
después de ver una película:
El Lago Azul. Y después
desperté en un solar. El día
quería olvidar a la noche entre
un montón de piedras oscuras.

Sí. Entre un montón de piedras oscuras.
Después se fueron mis compañeros. Y había
como el sabor intacto de otro día.
Y calles infantiles y futuras.

Después me entregué al Tiempo.

CUENTO DE INVIERNO

Cuando llegue el momento arreglaremos cuentas
en paz. Ya no podremos ganar ni perder nada.
Todo parecerá como recién vivido:
las ciudades; las hojas dormidas del cuaderno.

Tú me responderás con todo lo que sientas.
Será como un silencio hacia la madrugada.
Como un puente cruzado. Como algo que se ha ido.
Como un mar. El insomnio en un cuento de invierno.

Nos llenaremos de años entre cosas ausentes,
y la muerte será como un libro leído
donde la noche ambigua pone su gesto tierno.

Tú me harás el amor con las sombras, los dientes;
por los filos del aire recién estremecido.
Será como perderse en un cuento de invierno.

VOCACIÓN

Yo sé que lo que hago cada día
me justifica, aunque eso ya no importe.
Que, sin continuación, sigue su norte.
Sin mañana, su peso y su alegría.

Una noche de infancia verdadera
bajaré de puntillas, en pijama,
por la calle que duerme y que me llama,
como hace el tiempo por la primavera.

EL FANTASMA

Por el Paseo de los Tristes
han visto a Carlos Almira.
Las manos en los bolsillos.
Perdido entre los turistas.
La plaza, grande y callada.
Con un libro de poesías.

CARRETERAS SECUNDARIAS

Después de un año de aventuras
sin maestros y sin horarios,
por carreteras secundarias
y puticlubs de tres al cuarto,
me vi de pronto, estudiante
nocturno de Bachillerato,
con los poemas de don Luis
Cernuda y don Antonio Machado.

Del naufragio de aquellos días
he rescatado estos versos:
Pasa el tiempo como un pájaro
planeando en el silencio.
Y el invierno de los álamos,
me desnuda los recuerdos.

LOS FUTBOLINES

Jugamos en parejas.
Cómo ha pasado el tiempo.
Por el Geni exhausto,
el invierno.

Sobre las verdes lonas
los nubarrones negros.
El puente. Se hace tarde.
Frío. Recuerdo.

Sobre las lonas verdes,
se desbarata el viento.

EL MIRADOR

Las cosas, que no son nunca como pensamos,
huyen por un desierto donde el Tiempo se acuesta.
Delante de La Alhambra, una tarde como esta
que nunca volverá, tú y yo nos abrazamos.

Granada oscurecía cuando nos alejamos
del mirador. Un pájaro enmudecía en la cuesta.
Luego fueron la noche; las horas sin respuesta;
las calles; el silencio con que nos separamos.

La vida que no vuelve y nosotros vivimos,
se perdió como un eco por desiertos de plomo.
Aún flota somnolienta, su pausa suspendida,

al pie del mirador la Granada que fuimos;
el ciprés encantado con su pájaro romo;
San Nicolás arriba por su distancia huida.

CANCIÓN DE CAMINO

Camino Bajo de Huétor:
es una mañana fría;
voy al colegio; voy solo,
por una carreterita.

Mi padre, serio y callado;
mi madre con su desdicha;
voy enfrascado en mis cosas,
con una alegría íntima.

Las cosas duermen despiertas,
en una tinta amarilla.
Cuando sea mayor, quiero
ser un poeta de la vida.

Camino Bajo de Huétor,
en una mañana fría.

AUTORRETRATO 2

Uno siente, sin rencor, cada arañazo,
y sobre todo, la indiferencia y el frío
que van ocupando, paso a paso, su vida;
y saca fuerzas, no sabe de dónde,
para seguir siendo él mismo, pese a todo.

Me gustaría no hacer nada; vivir;
cruzar la calle con el paso más ligero;
y tirar al mar el fardo del pensamiento;
sentirme bien sólo por respirar.

Para cuidar al niño que me vive,
fui poeta por largos años oscuros.

EN ESTE CÉSPED

En este césped que ahora miras,
que casi pisas con los ojos,
jugué yo muchas tardes, muchas
mañanas, cuando yo era otro.

Algunas veces me caía
cuando intentaba hacer el trompo,
en este césped, ¿qué ha cambiado?,
que casi pisas con los ojos.

Luego me eché todo a la espalda,
y me fui donde se va todo.

EL TESORO

El mundo encierra un gran tesoro.
Sobre él escribe el poeta.
El poeta es como un músico.
Y el tesoro es el mundo mismo
que nadie ve, en el que nadie repara.

De otro modo no habría pobres
ni ricos; sanos ni enfermos;
felices ni desgraciados;
sólo el fulgor de cada momento
en los ojos y en las manos de todos.

ESTE POEMA

Será como si abrieras
una ventana a la calle. Será
como un espejo en un zaguán.
Como volver sobre los pasos.

Nunca volverás a ver
este poema. El libro
que tienes en las manos
ha echado a volar ya,
como tu vida.

DECLARACIÓN DE INTENCIONES

No me gusta dar clases.
Prefiero las estufas.
Es mejor hablar solo.
O tocar la bandurria.

Los barcos de papel.
La ensaladilla rusa.
Los quioscos de pipas.
O las noches de música.

La mala educación
es lo que más abunda.
Ministros y ministras.
Autoridades públicas.

Sí me gustan los libros.
El vino, las películas.
Las fuentes de los parques.
Los lápices con punta.

Pero mi verdadera vocación son las Bibliotecas
Municipales que se caen de puro sueño en los
fondos húmedos y enamorados de la nostalgia.

CORTA DESPEDIDA

Os he esperado mucho, pero ya
no puedo sujetarme, y me voy solo.
Da rabia hacerse viejo. Da rabia
perderos sin haberlo dicho todo.

Hubiéramos podido ser amigos;
sentarnos en un pollo o en un banco;
hablar; o cultivarnos en silencio,
cuando Granada tiembla hacia la tarde.

Gracias por correr. Cuando llegueis,
sentirme al menos en la cara,
como el relente de la noche.

SONETOS DE LA ALHAMBRA

I

Quiero tu cinta roja de murallas,
cifra de amor, remanso pensativo.
Tu ciprés con su pájaro furtivo,
cuando la tarde muere y te desmayas.

El agua que murmuras y te callas,
secreto fiel del muro y el olivo.
Y el paseo que, joven, descubrí
muy tarde, como el tiempo que nos deja.

Todo ha pasado, acepto. Soy olvido.
Quiero la tarde donde me perdí,
y el jazmín y el zumbido de la abeja.

El tiempo que nos deja dolorido,
cifra de amor que nunca comprendí,
por el remanso de la lejanía.

II

Y llorará en las tejas un pájaro salvaje (César Vallejo).

Nunca más te veré cómo venías
hasta mí, por las tardes con sus cielos.
Ni podré retenerte entre los hielos
que sorben nuestro tiempo y nuestros días.

Los flancos de tus torres altas, frías,
agitan las higueras, los albelos.
Y el pájaro minúsculo en su teja
se asoma hacia el Paseo de los Tristes.

Nunca más me verás cómo subía,
alfabeto de sombra y tarde vieja,
y silencio y amor donde persistes.

También me perderé en tu arqueología.
Y el pájaro minúsculo en su teja,
llorará hacia el Paseo de los Tristes.

EL RUMOR

Cuántos años hace que escucho
el mismo rumor sin prestarle
atención; golpes y voces confundidos
en la distancia; cuántos años
junto a la misma ventana; leyendo
o escribiendo; o simplemente escuchando
el mismo rumor sin hacerlo mío;
gastado, como la luz en la distancia.

CANCEL

Quiero abrir la ventana cuando la tarde lleva
con un sol casi frío, su cansancio del día;
y los ruidos, que vienen de lejos, se diría
anticipan la noche con una calma nueva.

La vida, que no es nunca como uno la espera,
me recoge en silencio como un campo nevado,
con un rumor de lluvia, casi de primavera.
Como en el Paraíso antes de Adán y Eva,

cuando la Historia pase su página sombría;
y la tarde, cansada, se parezca a otro día,
en la larga cadena -cadencia- que nos lleva.

Quiero abrir la ventana y que estés a mi lado:
porque la vida nunca es como uno la espera;
y dormir como el cielo sobre el campo acostado.

PRIMERA HORA

Es una iglesia como un barco.
Mi abuelo fuma en la terraza.
En las calles hay un rastro dulce
de espera, como de infancia.

Yo quiero echar a correr. Quiero
tocar los pinos de la plaza.
Las Parcas hilan con el aire
que menea las ramas.

SAXO Y PIANO

Mis días cotidianos y vendidos
¿para vivir?, se asoman a la hondura.
Dame tu voz, tu ráfaga que apura
la batalla del alma y los sentidos.

O déjame encogerme en tus latidos,
entre las hojas de tu voz oscura.
Noches del Eshavira. Madrugadas.
Estaciones de amor esquivo y duro.

No quiero la mañana con sus ruidos.
Su viña dura, de horas olvidadas.
Instrumento de amor. Columna pura.

Volver por mis caminos aprendidos.
Por tus noches de ráfagas heladas,
deshojar margaritas de locura.

EL MAR DE LA VIDA

Sólo quiero dormir. Ya no desenterrarme.
Desertar del momento: su tapiz intrincado.
Y hundir la cabeza en el mar de la vida.
Descansado de todo. Liberado del peso.
Sólo hundir la cabeza en el mar de la vida.

CANTO

En fin: habrá que escribir
sobre cómo se alargó la tarde
mientras dormías; con las primeras
horas de calor; y el vecindario
se volvió eco; pasado; rumor;
antes de entregarse al tiempo;
la distancia; y me llegó, feliz,
de la antigua unión del dios,
este canto.

AMOR 27

El amor, esa cárcel que tú sabes,
arrumba sus fachadas feas, viejas.
Déjame acariciarte las orejas,
como hace el mar oscuro con sus naves.

Me he empeñado en quererte y que me acabes.
Quiero bailar desnudo si me dejas.
Feliz como la brisa por las tejas.
Y otear el abismo que me labras.

Déjame acariciarte la cabeza.
Volar entre tus hojas y tus arcos.
Quiero saltar desnudo entre las cabras.

No despiertes. Aquí sólo hay tristeza.
Déjame que te arrulle con palabras.
Como hace el mar oscuro con los barcos.

MUGRE

El ventilador de techo:
removiendo el aire; cambiándolo
de sitio; como la mugre;
como las hojas secas de un jardín;
como los recuerdos.

CLASE DE MÚSICA
A Julia

Las manos sobre el teclado
van empujando las notas
indecisas, una tarde
de junio como las otras.

Limpia, como de una fuente
nueva, la música brota.
Las manos, aún infantiles,
van arrancando las notas.

Es una tarde, una tarde
de junio, como las otras.

JUVENTUD

A Charlie

Cuando tenía diecinueve o veinte años,
vivía solo con mis tías paternas;
cada tarde daba el mismo paseo
tras una jornada idéntica a las otras;
leía mucho; devoraba verdaderamente los libros;
y estudiaba y pensaba en el porvenir.
Sumido en la incertidumbre, pensaba en mi juventud:
¡Juventud divino tesoro, ya te vas para no volver!
Y levantaba la cabeza; y miraba a mi alrededor;
y veía los edificios, los coches, las tiendas. ¿Qué podía esperar de todo aquello,
tras largos años de estudio sino, con suerte, languidecer en un trabajo?
El mundo ya estaba repartido; estaba ocupado
por los que habían llegado antes que yo.
Y pensaba en mis padres; y en el hondo cariño que nos unía;
y en el mundo injusto y caduco que nos separaba.
Algún día debía llegar nuestro momento: aquellos
que supiesen esperar y persistir, ocuparían su lugar.
Entonces terminaba mi paseo entre los mismos árboles;
por las mismas calles donde jugaba de niño; y empezaba a oscurecer;
y sentía la calma de la noche, que no se repite nunca;
como si ya fuese viejo, y hubiese salido a dar una vuelta,
para recordar mi juventud.

AMOR

El arañazo, el zarpazo para algunos
de la vida, consiste en esperar,
cuando uno debería esforzarse al menos
en asomar un poco la cabeza
sobre el muro de las circunstancias.

Como si hubiera elegido estar ahí,
por puro amor.

LA MONEDA

¿Quién puede permanecer
en sí, como una moneda?

Todo se opone con fuerza
a que cuaje lo que somos.
Lo que en nosotros vive,
solo y por siempre.

BALANCE

¿No he sabido vivir? Me gustaría
haber sido más claro, más coherente.
Rico en frutos como el adolescente.
Como el niño sin fin que fui un día.

El amor es ahora todavía.
Cómo amanece silenciosamente
mientras escribo esto. De repente:
un pájaro; la calle; su armonía.

Cómo hubiera querido conocerte.
Conocer tus silencios, afligido.
¿No he sabido pasar hasta perderte?

El amor es ahora un tiempo huido.
Un color en la tarde en aguafuerte.
Como el mar que prepara nuestro olvido.

LA PLAZA

El sol alto, el mar,
habrá en La Laguna
una plaza con sombra,
con flores, donde podremos
otra vez densos, ricos,
no estropeados por la vida
aún, hablar.

LA COMETA

Si quieres, podemos ir a volar la cometa
antes de que empiece a oscurecer. Si hace aire,
con suerte, tras superar la primera zozobra,
subirá desdibujándose con la altura.

Podemos ir al descampado ahora, si quieres.
Por una o dos horas no habrá otra cosa en el mundo.
Yo sostendré la cruz y tú harás la carrera,
hasta que suba desdibujándose por la colina.

ISPHASAN

Nos cruzaremos un día
como hace años. Al verte
sentiré que te esperaba,
que te espero desde siempre.
Y me harás sitio, y nos iremos
callados, entre la gente.

CÓMO TE LLAMARÉ

Cómo te llamaré cuando, cansado,
cierre el libro a las horas de la tarde;
cuando el cielo recobre su silencio.
Te imagino en el patio, entre macetas;
por una calle rica y empinada.
Cómo responderé cuando me llames;
vuelta recuerdo; torre y balcón alto;
y el mar cansado, vuelva por mis horas;
y cierre el libro a las horas de la tarde.

EL MERCADO DE VALENCIA

Iremos desde la estación del tren
al Mercado Viejo.
Aún será de noche,
pero habrá mucha gente.

Iremos despacio,
callados, en nuestras cosas.

Tú me subirás el cuello del abrigo.
Nos abriremos paso entre los puestos,
y olerá a serrín y a flores.

EL VIVIENTE

Alguien tenía que hacerlo y yo lo hice.
No tenía derecho. No lo necesitaba.
Viví. Me despegué sobre el mar inconsciente.
Cada día llevaba su sabor escondido.

Alguien tenía que hacerlo. ¿Quién podía?
La soledad, el amor, me alumbraron a veces.
Viví por las palabras sobre un mar silencioso.
Cada día tenía su sabor escondido.

LA FOGATA

Estoy sentado en la Biblioteca;
estoy sentado; escribiendo;
solo; como cuando éramos muchachos;
en aquellos inviernos; y salíamos;
escribiendo y desamordazándome
del silencio, y la resaca del día;
entre desconocidos, y solo;
pero con un sentimiento íntimo y verdadero
de estar haciendo lo correcto; lo exacto;
lo único que podíamos hacer
para quitarnos el frío y el mundo de encima;
como cuando éramos niños,
y encendíamos una fogata en el campo.

EL ÚLTIMO DÍA

En la consulta del veterinario
había una pareja con un perro:
un animal grande y huesudo,
que no podía más con su alma.

Echado a los pies; con la cabeza
enorme entre las patas, soñaba:
con la calle recién regada y la finca
que en otro tiempo recorría señorialmente.

Entonces llegó su turno: su amo
lo cogió en brazos, y al borde de las lágrimas,
se lo llevó por última vez, allá dentro;
con una dignidad tranquila, envidiable;
con el mismo porte que debió tener antaño.

NI UNA SOLA LÁGRIMA

Un día
me acercaré a tocar la muerte;
me acercaré, incrédulo;
como la primera vez que te toqué.

Y tú estarás ahí,
aunque no lo sepas; -y será lo mejor-;
más allá de las lágrimas;
justo antes del olvido.

RUBAYAT

Ábreme. No estaré mucho tiempo.
Si quieres no diré nada. Cantaré.
No sé tocar ningún instrumento. Pero soy alegre.
Y tengo una risa contagiosa.

Pasemos la noche de la vida juntos.
Hasta que el día nos despierte.

EL MAESTRO

Aún estará el maestro
en el aula encantada;
sobre la mesa, el libro;
con un algo de infancia.

Cómo pasan los años;
cómo todo se acaba.
Y en el patio habrá un poco
de sol; de Dios; de nada.

LA ESPIGA

Soy la espiga, verde y pequeña,
que arrancabas por puro juego,
por distracción, en los ribazos
de las acequias y los caminos.
Por la delicia de la vida,
y el hechizo verde del horizonte,
entro ahora en tu poema.

HIMNO

Yo quiero vivir. ¡Vivir!
¿Yo? Un montón de cosas; de circunstancias;
de circunstancias que no elegí;
que me llevaron de un sitio a otro;
donde fui joven y pagué;
amores no correspondidos.
¡Yo quiero vivir, vivir!
Quiero tener los sueños que tú tienes;
y despertarme como tú despiertas;
estirarme despacio; abrir los ojos;
tanteando el calor, mirar el frío.
Amores no correspondidos
que aún arden,
en ciertos portales;
en calles por las que ya no paso.

UNA TARDE

Era una tarde de viernes.
Parece que lo estoy viendo.
Alrededor de la mesa,
se hizo de pronto el silencio.
Entraba la luz del patio.
Era una tarde de invierno.

A MI MAESTRO O MAESTRA

Como si una mirada, un momento,
pudiese descubrir lo que somos
-nuestro destino-, una mañana
de invierno, entre las filas de niños
adormilados, tú soñaste quién era yo;
-nada del otro mundo, por otra parte-;
seguramente entonces ni te percataste; y después
de inmediato, ya no volviste a reparar en mí.

Sin embargo, los años no han pasado;
pues la verdad es como un agua inmóvil;
y aunque ya no recuerde tu cara;
ni tu voz pueda tocarme; ni tu gesto;
a través de los vastos espacios desiertos, te debo todo lo que soy;
lo mucho o lo poco que ha aflorado de mí desde ese momento;
en la rápida sucesión de los días.

Si vivimos, aunque sólo sea un instante;
y somos auténticos; nosotros; es porque alguien
nos miró de una vez para siempre; amorosamente;
como tú lo hiciste conmigo; y al instante siguiente
apartó los ojos distraídos; y volvió a colmar el silencio;
con la voz y los gestos comunes; destinados a borrarse:
como el reflejo de los árboles en el agua;
o como la lluvia en la madrugada.

LLUVIA

Lluvia, despierta
la cansada ciudad.

EQUILIBRIO

Algunas tardes eran
tan intensas, que parecía
que el equilibrio del mundo iba,
estaba a punto de romperse.

Entonces nos callábamos,
perdidos en nuestros pensamientos.
Perdidos para siempre.

LA REALIDAD Y EL DESEO

Me despierto de pronto, sin razones.
Solo. Vivo. La casa me conoce.
De la noche un escalofrío, un roce
amoroso, recorre las habitaciones.
Toda, toda la soledad que me impones
se resuelve de pronto en puro goce.
Leo tus poemas. Hay como un desbroce
de amor, de madrugada, en los rincones.
Me despierto. No sé qué haré mañana.
Solo. Vivo. Con mis meditaciones.
Y el sol pone su día en la ventana.
Leo tus poemas como si volviera
de otros años, con una luz lejana.
Con una luz que no nos reconoce.

CANTAR

Lo que yo siento se puede
decir de muchas maneras.
Viví como pude. Ahora
siento que todo me deja.

La tarde en el vecindario
va preparando mi ausencia.
Alta, sobre el cielo frío,
tiene un no sé qué de estrella.

Lo que yo siento, se puede
cantar de muchas maneras.

CALLE POETA MANUEL DE GÓNGORA

Cómo me gusta pasear por aquí
entre semana;
pararme a ver las tiendas;
sentarme en una cafetería
sin prisas; darte la mano
sin decir nada; y andar,
andar, andar; cómo me gusta.

HOMENAJE AL POETA SALVATORE QUASIMODO

Por las tapias disparejas
entre las casas, invierno.
Todo se desvanece, menos
tu recuerdo de roca.
Fuerza, adolescencia,
en la luz perfumada.

VATICINIO

Despertaremos un día
diferente, como todos.
Nos parecerá lo mismo
la habitación, el escorzo
de la calle en la ventana.
Algo perdido, muy hondo,
nos llamará desde el niño
que fuimos.

JUSTO ANTES DE ANOCHECER

Cuando el río empezaba a quedarse callado,
daban luz a las farolas, todas feas e iguales;
y soñábamos; las calles; los oscuros portales;
era como un rumor lejano, olvidado;
era como si todo ya estuviese parado;
como la oscuridad que veremos un día.

CONCIENCIA

No sé porqué he vivido,
y sí sé porqué he vivido.
Cuando no lo sé, me siento otra persona.
Pero cuando lo sé, me atisbo
como un árbol tras una tapia.
Y me veo en un camino,
en una noche llena de estrellas.

RETRATO

Soy un hombre a medio hacer.
Empecé muchas cosas.
Quería dejar un mundo mejor.
Ahora quiero vivir, como el poeta.
Muchas noches escucho el viento
cuando no me puedo dormir.
Quería viajar, pero me quedé en el piso
lleno de ecos de niños.
Sé menos de lo que nunca sabré.

AUTOELEGÍA

Hace una tarde hermosa de febrero,
y la vida es un vuelo delicado,
frágil. Como si no hubiese empezado,
se acaba todo, todo lo que quiero.

Como un golpe de mar, duro y certero,
el tiempo me empujó, desarbolado.
La juventud, un viento huracanado,
me deja su perfume verdadero.

Me trajo su perfume denso, oscuro.
Y la vida fue el gesto donde callas,
para no despertar antes del día.

Como un golpe de mar, incierto y puro,
ante la muerte fue mi fantasía
como una ciudadela sin murallas.

EL PASEO

Una mañana, hace tiempo,
por el Paseo del Darro
íbamos juntos, y tú
me quisiste decir algo.
Aún me parece sentir
el apretón de tu mano.
Luego el rumor de la calle,
nos fue envolviendo, callados.
Una mañana hace tiempo,
me quisiste decir algo.

LA NIÑA

En un refugio, en plena guerra,
bombardeos, incendios,
una niña muy pequeña
canta en la oscuridad. Canta sola.
Y toda la noche de la guerra
retrocede en silencio. Y se abre
en torno a ella, menuda, frágil, sola,
como un claro de otro mundo,
¡qué diferente de este, qué diferente!
en el fondo del refugio.

NIEVA

En el silencio de la guerra
a veces nieva, y el campo
se endurece como los hombres,
las mujeres, los niños.

Y la nieve duda un momento
antes de tocar los cuerpos, las calles,
como cuando todo vivía.

HOMENAJE A GLORIA FUERTES

Para ponerme al corriente,
pagué mis facturas de amor.
Luego me acosté y dormí,
con la conciencia bien limpia,
escuchando el camión de la basura.

UNA TARDE

Es verano. Podemos ir al cine.
O quedarnos en casa, si prefieres.
Buscar una película. Hacer algo
con los pájaros tristes de la tarde.

Piensa que envejecemos. Y que al tiempo
sólo lo ven los gatos y los niños.
Cómo canta el rumor en la distancia.
Nunca más, nunca más, repite todo.

O podemos leer. No sé. Hacer algo
con los pájaros tristes de la tarde.

LA PLAZA

Aún seguirá la misma plaza
de las Pasiegas, con su ángel.
Y te mirará sin verte,
sobre la otra, cuando pases.

Las luces recién encendidas
en torno, irán oscureciéndose
las calles cuando pases, solo,
rumiando tus primeros versos.

DÍAS

Días feroces como puños
de americanas, quemados,
que se quedaron frías, oscilando
hace mucho, en una puerta.

Que nadie querrá reclamar
cuando el tiempo feliz vuelva.
Hinchados como globos. Perdidos
en el remolino indisciplinado.

Este es mi certificado de paternidad:
sois míos para siempre.

EL VIAJERO

Me da vértigo volverme,
como si fuera en un tren-bala;
y el paisaje quisiera llorar;
y el tren sólo pensara en pararse
en una estación cualquiera;
en medio del invierno.

QUERIDO CUERPO

Querido cuerpo:
Gracias por estar ahí;
por traerme y llevarme
todos estos años.

Cómo me hubiera gustado
conocerte mejor.
Pero recuerda: En esto
estamos juntos hasta el fin.

Ahora toca ser humo
y callada brisa.

EL EXTRAÑO

Decidió no ser como los otros
para no cumplir años ajenos,
y no pagarlos con su alma.
Se hizo poeta
sólo por el gusto de verse
cuando un día lo sacasen de su casa,
desde el portal de enfrente, al fin
solo, desnudo y huérfano
por la misma calle que cruzara tantas veces
sin saber que vivía,
como el sol y el aire.

PASEO

Voy despacio y solo.
Me gustaría verme
como el agua que pasa,
cansada por el cielo,
en un olvido dorado.

SAUDADE

El fin de la amistad y la muerte del brillo de los ojos. Yeats

Todo lo que eras lo quisiste
sin darte cuenta. Cada hora
vuelve con todo lo que fuiste,
y se agolpa en lo que eres ahora.

Lo demás no es importante.
Sólo cuenta lo que se ha vivido.
Y el oro de la tarde errante.
Y el brillo de los ojos.

MOZART

La vida juega con la muerte,
pero las notas se le escapan.
Ella escucha la música,
y la tarde se esconde por su cara.

Por las columnas del patio
suben las escalas.
     Ella escucha
cómo juega la vida con la muerte,
pero las notas se le escapan.

Y hay una tristeza que casi parece alegría.

ROMANCE DEL LIBERADO

"Cómo le diremos al mar que nos ahogamos en la tierra" (Grafiti
del puerto de Árgel).

Cómo diremos al mar
que nos ahogamos en tierra.
Los padres se hacían viejos.
Se nos cerraban las puertas.
En las ciudades sin alma,
sólo florecía la niebla.
Y nos fuimos por un sueño.
Por no agachar la cabeza.
Para volver algún día,
como las aves que vuelan.

PRIMERA HORA

El cambio sutil del tiempo
más fresco por las mañanas
al principio, anunciaba un giro
completo, en rosas y constelaciones,
y buscábamos un libro para conjurar
las noches del invierno inminente.

Había una mosca parada
en la cara del abuelo, y otra
en las manos del padre,
que vivía de sus sueños, lejos, en el campo
sumergido por el agua y la distancia,
por el pantano de los Bermejales.

Toda nuestra infancia fue eso:
ese momento primero de la mañana;
y el zumbido terso y tardío
del aire rasgado, vuelto rasguño desolado,
advertencia de las horas del invierno.

Y otra volaba en la nariz y los labios
cantando el tiempo anunciado.

DÍAS

Un día me parece
que vienes, y salimos
casi de madrugada,
por el portal dormido.

Salimos en silencio.
El primer cigarrillo,
antes de beber nada
es el mejor, decimos.

En la calle desierta,
oscila un farolillo.

DOBLE FILA

Estoy escuchando música
solo, en el coche parado.
Estoy escuchando música,
con el corazón helado.

La gente pasa. En el frío
de las caras no se ve
la sombra verde del río,
el tiempo que ya se fue.

Solo, en el coche parado,
estoy escuchando música
con el corazón helado.

LOS MÚSICOS

Una tarde. Oscurece.
En la plaza unos músicos
guardan sus instrumentos.
En el aire aún vibran
los últimos acordes.

Antes de apagarse del todo
se ofrecen, ya sin público,
solos, entre los débiles
contornos que se esfuman,
felices e inefables.

AUTORRETRATO 3

Una gorra arrugada
y casi amarilla, enmarca
con la barba, la cabeza
donde la cara languidece.

La mirada hundida
en torno a las ojeras,
atenta aún a los filos
de la rosa invisible.

SESENTA

Tanto tiempo escribí que no me acuerdo.
Todo se me ha escurrido suavemente.
Cerca de los sesenta uno se siente
más proclive al amor que al desacuerdo.

Me quedo solo y siento que me pierdo.
Quiero gritar y callo nuevamente.
Que he perdido mi nombre dulcemente.
Y hay un jardín antiguo que recuerdo.

Tanto tiempo y tan poca poesía.
Un abuelo inventor y un padre muerto.
Un ayer por llenar que se me aleja.

Y el huracán de la melancolía.
Cerca de los sesenta uno está abierto
al amor, como al mundo que lo deja.

CANTAR DE AMIGO

Es una mañana sola,
como todas las mañanas.
Las manos en los bolsillos,
voy por una calle larga.

Echo de menos tu voz,
y tus manos, y tu cara;
y la forma que tenías
de callarte cuando hablabas.

Es una mañana antigua
como todas las mañanas.
Las manos en los bolsillos,
voy por una calle larga.

JERUSALEM

Cuántas horas de estudio, de trabajo
paciente, fueron necesarias;
de atención; cuántos días
de soledad, robados a sus noches;
al sueño; a la resignación tranquila
en su paz aparente; porque el alma
te aguijoneaba con la antigua pregunta
del Evangelio; cuántas ciudades;
porque el agua volviese a su frescura,
del amargo trabajo de los hombres;
y el pájaro, sin sombra, la cantase
como un día.

AMOR URBANO

Vamos a hablar. Después la discoteca
soltará nuestros cuerpos, bien templados.
La madrugada irá por los tejados,
como ginebra azul y rama seca.

Al besarnos, un gusto de manteca
fruncirá nuestros ojos estrellados.
Al morder, nuestros dientes afilados,
encontrarán su savia amarga y hueca.

Antes de que las calles aún dormidas,
con las Parcas que tejen nuestras vidas,
pongan en entredicho nuestra dicha.

Vamos a desnudarnos, exaltados.
Y el tiempo dormirá como una bicha
de madrugada, sobre los tejados.

PETICIÓN

En un piso del Zaidín,
cerca del estadio de fútbol,
vivían mis tres tías.

Tú, que lees esto,
siéntelo y hazles justicia
con tu emoción.

SAXO

Escuché una música que venía
desde la plaza de la catedral,
que quería echarse en el aire tranquilo,
donde ya empezaba a oscurecer.
Me acerqué al extranjero, (¿cómo sabía
que era extranjero?), que tocaba el saxo.
Y estuve escuchándolo un buen rato, de olvido
y penumbra. Hasta que aquella música desconocida
entró en mi alma, (quería echarse en el aire tranquilo
donde ya empezaba la noche).
Y se quedó allí, encallada, para siempre.

EL GRAN RÍO

Si te asaltara la duda a cada paso,
de si lo que has pensado, en realidad
no lo habrás dicho también en voz alta;
como cuando uno habla en sueños;
en una calle; o en una plaza; o solo;
en el fondo de un autobús; o en un bar;
para que el sigilo indiscreto de tus ensueños;
o tus gestos, no te traicionen (quién sabe quién podría oírlo);
y prefirieras no tener pensamientos propios;
¿al fin y al cabo, de quién son los pensamientos?;
no por miedo, sino por modestia; por convencionalismo;
para no ser un bicho raro; entonces sopesa bien esto:
todo aquello a lo que tendrás que renunciar;
a entrever en la gran calma de tus pensamientos;
a oír en esa gran calma, el río de la vida y su pájaro;
lo que una vez te emocionó y te hizo lo que eres.

RECUERDO

Son los años setenta.
Un día entre semana.
Una luz cenicienta,
entra por la ventana.

¿Llueve? Leo tumbado.
En la tarde madura,
flota como algo usado,
sobre la calle oscura.

Son los años setenta.
De la tarde lejana,
una luz cenicienta,
entra por la ventana.

ELEGÍA

Quién está escribiendo esto. Ahora sé
que el mundo nunca volverá a juntarse por tus ojos.
Y aunque parezca trabado por otros, "nunca más"
ya está escrito en cada calle y en cada perfume.

La muerte ha desanudado lo que tus ojos unían.
Y yo lloro el trabajo de todos los espejos.

LAS SOMBRAS

Sé que antes de morir, viste
con miedo, con asombro de niña,
huellas ligeras en el aire, sombras
del mundo invisible. En los cerrados
contornos de las calles en cuesta,
que insinúan el espesor del día.

Muchas veces, echado en la oscuridad,
yo también he sentido como
un gato se echaba entre mis piernas, remoto,
con todo lo que nos separaba y nos unía:
las casas en paz, al anochecer;
el son con su inmemorial tristeza.

BAR MADRID

Hace frío. En el café,
música de los ochenta.
Hay una tristeza antigua,
varada sobre las mesas.
Y hay una alegría antigua,
como si no se sintiera.
Afuera, la muchedumbre
busca una rosa en la niebla.

UN HOMBRE

Un hombre solo, despacio,
con su alegría y su pena.
En la avenida los olmos
verdes, con sus hojas nuevas.

ELEGÍA

Cómo le diremos al mar que nos ahogamos en tierra.
A la tierra, que tenemos nuestras raíces en el viento.
Cómo le diremos al fuego que estamos hechos de noche.
Cómo parece quieto todo lo que nos mueve, solo.
Y cómo gira todo en el espacio sin aire del pasado.
Como la dulzura del verano dentro de la sombra que tiembla.
Como las imágenes del invierno intactas dentro de la rosa.

Qué cansancio y qué anhelo de volver con los padres.
A la calle doctor Zamenhoff. A la plaza del Mercado.
Y volver a conocerse por el Puerto Gris de Santa Cruz.
Con otro nombre y con otro corazón para inaugurar el silencio.

Desde las azoteas aún pueden verse los barcos entre los
perdigones.
Y cómo se mueve todo y nos deja parados y desconocidos.
En medio de nosotros donde hay una tarde verde de nostalgia.
Yo he hecho mi camino incompleto. Vuelvo a leer mis libros.
Paseo. Me gusta nuestra calle. A veces hablo solo.
Y los árboles me cubren, me arropan con sus grandes hojas.
Y cierro los ojos y me veo aún, siempre de niño en el pueblo.

Cuando las Parcas me llamen;
cuando me llamen las Parcas;
en el remolino negro
les enseñaré tu cara.

EL TUMULTO

Quiero hacerte el amor con un soneto.
Que nos vea la estrella matutina.
Cuando el saxo enmudezca por completo,
y la noche se esfume en cada esquina.

El blues encerrará nuestro amor quieto
en un beso, como una mandarina.
Y el humo esconderá nuestro secreto.
Y el alcohol dormirá nuestra rutina.

La vida nunca vuelve ni perdona
a quienes no se pierden en un beso.
Hazme el amor y sé tú mi madona.

Porque el fin del amor consiste en eso.
En roer cada día como un hueso,
en un tumulto que nos abandona.

TODO. METAFÍSICA DEL POETA.

Donde se acaban el espacio y el tiempo.
En cada nota callada en el enjambre.
Donde el alma y el cuerpo se sostienen.
En la música en la oscuridad del teatro.
Está todo lo que he buscado y he vivido.
Como las hormigas en el viejo tronco.
En el amor rugoso de su contacto.

EL LLANTO

El agua fría y verde
del tiempo, nos arrastra.
¿Qué vas a hacer, Pepita,
cuando no tengas lágrimas?
Llorando, siempre llorando
un llanto que no acaba.
Frío y grande, de niño.
Que no acaba.

ELEGÍA

A Mari

Mari, ya no veremos
más series los domingos.
Todo se irá callando,
quedándose vacío.

Aunque parezca igual,
nada será lo mismo.
Como si entre nosotros
se abriera un precipicio.

Lloro, pero no vuelves,
como no vuelve el niño.
Por los relojes sólo
madruga el amarillo.

SIN NOTICIAS

El poeta Tao-Han dejó unos versos
y ninguna noticia de su vida,
fuera de la época Tang a la que pertenecen,
tan llena de sucesos, reales y legendarios.

Debió ocuparlo tan intensamente componerlos,
debieron absorverlo tanto, que olvidó anotar
la fecha y el lugar de su nacimiento,
entre otras andanzas de su vida,
así como la fecha y las circunstancias de su muerte.

Como florece sencillamente el campo.

ÍNDICE   *página*

Carlos Almira Picazo, 1965. Escritor y poeta español.